BLAST SINKS
U.S. SUBMARINE NEAR BOSTON

A mysterious explosion sank the U.S. navy submarine **Swordfish** four miles outside Boston harbor at 2 PM today.

A young woman survivor was picked up by a private yacht cruising in the neighborhood at the time. The survivor seemed dazed by the shock, and when the yacht brought her ashore in Boston, she broke away and escaped. She has not been found.

It is reported this girl leaped from the submarine some moments before the explosion.

There is also a rumor that the girl wore a portion of a suit of ancient armor, and that the few words she uttered were couched in accents of the Sixteenth Century in England.

It is feared the submarine sank in water too deep for a rescue to be affected.

Naval officials are reluctant to discuss the matter.

THE SUBMARINE MYSTERY

THE MAN OF BRONZE
THE THOUSAND-HEADED MAN
METEOR MENACE
THE POLAR TREASURE
BRAND OF THE WEREWOLF
THE LOST OASIS
THE MONSTERS
THE LAND OF TERROR
THE MYSTIC MULLAH
THE PHANTOM CITY
FEAR CAY
QUEST OF QUI
LAND OF ALWAYS-NIGHT
THE FANTASTIC ISLAND
MURDER MELODY
THE SPOOK LEGION
THE RED SKULL
THE SARGASSO OGRE
PIRATE OF THE PACIFIC
THE SECRET IN THE SKY
COLD DEATH
THE CZAR OF FEAR
FORTRESS OF SOLITUDE
THE GREEN EAGLE
THE DEVIL'S PLAYGROUND
DEATH IN SILVER
THE MYSTERY UNDER
  THE SEA
THE DEADLY DWARF
THE OTHER WORLD
THE FLAMING FALCONS
THE ANNIHILIST
THE SQUEAKING GOBLINS
MAD EYES

THE TERROR IN THE NAVY
DUST OF DEATH
RESURRECTION DAY
HEX
RED SNOW
WORLD'S FAIR GOBLIN
THE DAGGER IN THE SKY
MERCHANTS OF DISASTER
THE GOLD OGRE
THE MAN WHO SHOOK THE
  EARTH
THE SEA MAGICIAN
THE MEN WHO SMILED NO
  MORE
THE MIDAS MAN
LAND OF LONG JUJU
THE FEATHERED OCTOPUS
THE SEA ANGEL
DEVIL ON THE MOON
HAUNTED OCEAN
THE VANISHER
THE MENTAL WIZARD
HE COULD STOP THE
  WORLD
THE GOLDEN PERIL
THE GIGGLING GHOSTS
POISON ISLAND
THE MUNITIONS MASTER
THE YELLOW CLOUD
THE MAJII
THE LIVING FIRE MENACE
THE PIRATE'S GHOST
THE SUBMARINE
  MYSTERY

THE SUBMARINE MYSTERY

A DOC SAVAGE ADVENTURE

BY KENNETH ROBESON

BANTAM BOOKS · TORONTO · NEW YORK · LONDON

A NATIONAL GENERAL COMPANY

THE SUBMARINE MYSTERY
*A Bantam Book / published by arrangement with
The Condé Nast Publications Inc.*

PRINTING HISTORY
Originally published in DOC SAVAGE *Magazine June 1938*
Bantam edition published August 1971

*Bantam Books are published by Bantam Books, Inc., a National
General company. Its trade-mark, consisting of the words "Bantam
Books" and the portrayal of a bantam, is registered in the United
States Patent Office and in other countries. Marca Registrada.
Bantam Books, Inc., 666 Fifth Avenue, New York, N.Y. 10019.*

PRINTED IN THE UNITED STATES OF AMERICA

CONTENTS

Chapter I

THE SUBMARINE MYSTERY

THE story made the front pages of most of the newspapers. A typical headline and bulletin was the one appearing in the *Planet*, a morning newspaper in Tulsa, Oklahoma. It read:

BLAST SINKS U. S. SUBMARINE
NEAR BOSTON

A mysterious explosion sank the U. S. navy submarine *Swordfish* four miles outside Boston harbor at 2 P.M. to-day.

A young woman survivor was picked up by a private yacht cruising in the neighborhood at the time. The survivor seemed dazed by the shock, and when the yacht brought her ashore in Boston, she broke away and escaped. She has not been found.

It is reported this girl leaped from the submarine some moments before the explosion.

There is also a rumor that the girl wore a portion of a suit of ancient armor, and that the few words she uttered were couched in accents of the Sixteenth Century in England.

It is feared the submarine sank in water too deep for a rescue to be affected.

Naval officials are reluctant to discuss the matter.

This was the story which appeared in the Tulsa newspaper. The only difference between this story and the others which were printed was a matter of wording and color. Some papers printed a dramatic eyewitness story by the yachtsmen, telling how the sub had been literally ripped from end to end by the blast.

There were also fuller descriptions of the young woman who had been rescued. Her unusual attire—the portion of a suit of ancient armor—came in for comment. It was remarkable. It was unusual for a woman to be on a U-boat. And for the woman to be dressed in the fighting garb of another century was puzzling.

1

The newspapers guessed at various explanations, the most prevalent one being that the young woman was a professional artist's model dressed for some kind of publicity photograph.

All the descriptions mentioned the look of terror which had been in the girl's eyes.

And all the newspaper stories mentioned the fact that naval officials were reluctant to discuss the affair.

They were reluctant for a very good reason.

A rear admiral at the Brooklyn Navy Yard was the first one to discover an incredible fact about the submarine disaster. He read a radiogram to the effect that the U. S. navy U-boat *Swordfish* had blown up.

"Hell's bells!" he bellowed.

The U. S. navy had a submarine named *Swordfish*. But the *Swordfish* was lying at the Panama Canal. Or was it? The rear admiral sent a volley of radio messages. It was. The U. S. navy submarine *Swordfish* was at the Panama Canal. It was really there. Nothing had happened to it.

"Must have been another one of our subs that sank," the rear admiral muttered.

He sent another batch of radio messages. The replies apprised him of an astounding fact: Every single U. S. navy submarine could be accounted for! Not a U-boat was missing!

The submarine which had sunk was obviously not a U. S. navy sub.

"Darn yachtsmen must have made a mistake identifying it," the rear admiral decided.

He flew to Boston and personally questioned the yachtsmen who had observed the blast. He left that conference holding the back of his neck. The yachtsmen had positively seen *U. S. S. Swordfish* on the submersible. The U-boat had absolutely been flying American colors. The rescued girl had certainly worn part of a suit of ancient armor, and her few words had been spoken in Sixteenth-Century English.

All of which was a headache.

THE American people and the American newspapers are prone to credit their government, their army and their navy with little or no ability as diplomats. For some contrary reason, they like to insist that whenever a mess comes up, the Americans are sure to put their foot in it. At the drop of a hat, they will declare an American diplomat is no diplomat at all. It now developed that this was a slight mistake.

The world at the moment was in one of those stages where it is called a powder keg. There was an undeclared war or two going on in Europe; the Japanese were swallowing another chunk of China, and various dictators were shaking hands with each other and making faces at the rest of the universe.

Fully a dozen so-called civilized nations had teeth and claws all set to fly at each other. All they needed was something to give a little push.

If somebody's submarine had been blown up, that might be just the little push that would start world fireworks.

There was a tense conference of U. S. government bigwigs. No one ever told exactly what was said there.

But the U. S. navy submarine *Swordfish* lying in Panama suddenly had its name changed to *Trigger Fish*.

The navy did not deny paternity of the submarine *Swordfish* which sank near Boston. True, the navy did not seem to coöperate in its usual hearty fashion with the newspapers. It did not, for instance, publish a list of names of those who had died in the disaster. As the rear admiral said privately, the U. S. navy had no way of communicating with the dead to get the information.

At any rate, no European or Asiatic war started over the matter.

If any of the newspapers smelled a rat, they did not manage to dig the rodent out of its hole.

The U. S. Naval Intelligence, the Feds, and other government-sleuthing agencies did conduct an intensive hunt for the girl who had escaped—the girl with the armor and the look of horror. They made just one discovery:

A girl wearing armor and a look of horror on her face had stolen a fast airplane from a flying field near Boston. The plane had contained enough gas to fly to South America, Ireland, Spain, Canada or other places.

The armor-wearing girl took the plane off in the direction of the South Atlantic, which was no help. There was nothing she could fly to in that direction.

New York was only one of the places where the government agencies kept a sharp watch for her.

Chapter II

TROUBLE BUMP

WHO said that great oaks grow from little acorns isn't important. Who said it had no bearing on Clark Savage, Jr.

What did have a bearing on Doc Savage was a piece of gray rock. No great oak grew from this gray rock, but what did grow was a great deal more interesting.

Doc was driving along a Long Island road and saw the gray rock where it had no business to be, geologically. Among many other things, Doc was a geologist, experts admitting that he knew as much about rocks as almost any other man. That gray rock was as irregular as a polar bear walking around in Florida.

Doc stared at the rock. So he did not see the two men in the passing truck. The men were blowing their noses in big bandanna handkerchiefs, a ruse to hide their faces. The truck whipped in front of Doc's car and stopped.

Doc stamped brakes and stopped.

The truck was a huge van. The back end of this suddenly dropped. It became an inclined ramp.

A car promptly crashed into Doc's machine from the rear. Doc Savage's automobile was knocked scooting up the ramp into the van.

The back of the van closed up tightly.

The truck lurched into motion.

Doc Savage dived out of his car. He was much taller than an average man, but so balanced in development that the fact was not evident until he stood close to some object to which his size could be compared.

Tropic suns had given his skin a pronounced bronze coloration, and his hair was straight, of a bronze color only slightly darker than his skin, and fitted remarkably like a metal skull-cap.

4

Doc's eyes searched the van. His eyes were probably the bronze man's most unusual feature. They were like pools of flake gold, never inactive, always stirring, and possessing a compelling power that was distinctly hypnotic.

The van was sheathed—floor, walls and ceiling—with armor-plate steel. Getting out of a jail would be simple compared to getting out of this.

Doc Savage made a small sound which was an unconscious thing he did in reaction to moments of intense mental effort, or puzzled surprise.

The sound was a trilling; low, exotic, as fantastic as the night wind around the eaves of a haunted house. It was made somehow in the bronze man's throat. Its strangest quality was the fact that it seemed to come from everywhere in the van.

Doc SAVAGE sat down on the running board of his car to reflect. Also to eliminate possible explanations for what had just happened.

In five minutes, he was mystified, and after ten minutes had passed, he was completely at a loss. He had no idea why he'd been kidnaped, or where his captors might be taking him.

Doc Savage was not unaware that he had been for some time acquiring a world-wide reputation as a modern scientific Galahad who went about the globe righting wrongs and punishing evil-doers. He did not work for pay. He had a source of fabulous wealth, gained in one of his early adventures.

Since he did not have to make a living out of his strange profession, he could select any crime that interested him, the result being that any criminal was likely to find the man of bronze on his trail.

Doc had better than a sprinkling of potential enemies, and they had a habit of trying to dispose of him unexpectedly. Possibly a potential enemy was trying something now.

The big van rolled along fast, exhaust throbbing, tires wailing on concrete pavement.

Doc got a hammer out of his tool kit and began to beat on the front of the van. Sparks flew. Finally a tiny barred window opened in the front of the van.

A hand displayed a small cylindrical metal object. The

article was equipped with a spout similar to a perfume atom-
izer, but without the squeeze bulb.

A voice said, "Know'st thou what this be?"

Two things immediately interested the bronze man: The
first was the manner in which the words were spoken. The
speaker used the delivery and pronunciation of an actor
doing a bit of Shakespeare.

The second thing of interest was the device which the man
was displaying. Doc recognized it as a type of tear-gas gun
which was sold in novelty stores and could be bought by anybody with fifteen dollars to spend for such a thing. He did
not care to have it start spouting.

"The idea," Doc said, "seems to be that you are in a
position to make it disagreeable for me."

A second voice spoke from the driver's seat.

"You got it right, pal," this man said. "Cut out the racket,
or Henry will squirt tear gas in there with you."

Doc Savage decided there was certainly nothing Shake-
spearean about the speech of the second man. Doc stooped
and looked through the aperture to determine how many
men were in the driver's compartment of the truck.

There were only two men.

THE man holding the tear-gas gun had been called Henry
by the other man.

Henry was a very long, lean article, chiefly notable for
his ample ears and the expression of a fellow who has just
taken a bite of apple which he suddenly suspects may contain
a worm.

This expression of finding life a bitter pill to taste was
apparently a habitual one with Henry. Additionally, Henry
had very red hair which looked as if it had no life, like the
hair in a very old wig. Henry was about forty.

" 'Tis best thee be peaceable!" Henry said gloomily.

Doc Savage then gave his attention to the second of his
two captors.

He saw a man who had a warped nose, snaggly teeth, black
hair as curly as bedsprings, and a skin that would have been
appropriate on a rhinoceros. In his necktie, this man wore
a stick pin containing a pearl that was large, yellowish and
obviously artificial. He had a very red face. His age might

be thirty, but it was hard to tell about such a man. He was very wide for his height.

"Have you got a name?" Doc asked him.

"Pipe down and get your schnozzle out of that hole!" the wide man said.

He had a deep and coarse voice; when he spoke, it was about equivalent to hearing a canary croak like a frog.

"I do not understand this," Doc said.

The man said, "Curiosity is good for you!" Then he slammed the window shut, and the truck continued on its way.

Doc Savage climbed into his car, apparently not greatly concerned. He felt under the dashboard until he located a hidden switch, which he turned on, and the result was a hum of a radio warming up. It was not a conventional car radio; this one was a short-wave transmitter and receiver.

"Hello, Monk!" Doc said into the microphone.

Almost at once, a voice replied, "Yes, Doc?"

It was a very small voice; it might have belonged to a boy, or a midget.

"Monk," Doc Savage said, "an unusual thing has happened. I have just encountered two gentlemen, and one of them seems to insist on talking like Shakespeare."

"Like what?"

"Shakespeare."

"I don't get you, Doc."

"It is a strange story, ending with a slight predicament," the bronze man explained.

Chapter III

THE FISH AND THE BAIT

"MONK," otherwise known as Lieutenant Colonel Andrew Blodgett Mayfair, was a man who was somewhat ridiculous in two or three ways—being amazing in appearance, shorter than many men, wider than most men, and more hairy than almost any man; and he had a face that was something to start babies laughing, the little tikes probably not thinking it human, but something funny made for their amusement.

As "Ham" frequently remarked: if worst came to worst, Monk might get a job posing for Halloween funny-face masks. "Ham" was Brigadier General Theodore Marley Brooks, lawyer and sartorial artist.

Ham and Monk had three things in common: they both belonged to Doc Savage's crew of five; they both had unusual animals for pets, and each one liked to quarrel with the other. They quarreled interminably. It went on when they ate, fought, or made love. Nothing seemed to interfere with their squabbling.

As for Monk, it was not likely he would ever have to pose for Halloween funny-faces to make a living. Monk was world-renowned as a chemist. Whenever a big corporation hired him as a consulting chemist, they usually paid him a fee as large as the salary of the president of the United States. That was the most ridiculous thing about Monk. His head did not look as if it had room for a spoonful of brains.

Monk leaned back lazily, put his feet on the inlaid table in the reception room of Doc Savage's skyscraper headquarters in New York City, and spoke into the microphone. His mind was at peace, for he had made a mistake—by "predicament," he supposed Doc meant something minor. Doc did not sound excited.

"Here's a good one, Doc," Monk chuckled. "Chemistry, that

blasted runt ape pet of Ham's, has been devilin' my pet pig, Habeas Corpus, for weeks. But the worm finally turned. Habeas got hold of Chemistry and blamed near ate a leg off him, and the ape has been roostin' on the chandelier all day, afraid to——"

"I've been kidnaped!" Doc advised.

Monk's feet fell off the desk. *"What?"*

Doc Savage could hardly have been as calm mentally as he was physically. He was a prisoner in the van, which meant trouble. Serious trouble, conceivably. If it was not serious, the captors probably wouldn't have gone to such elaborate pains to get him.

The bronze man had been speaking in a low voice. His captors might discover at any moment that he was talking over a radio from inside the van. Or the van might reach its destination. Haste seemed advisable.

"You and Ham," Doc said, "might sort of trail along."

Monk's voice was an astonished squeak over the radio. "Trail where? What's goin' on?"

Doc explained with small words that he had been bumped, car and all, into a big van, and that the van was now taking him to an unknown destination.

"And the way one of them talks," the bronze man finished, "is the queerest thing of all."

"Way he talks?"

"He uses Sixteenth-Century English."

"He what?"

"He sounds like Shakespeare."

"Just what kind of gag," Monk demanded, "is this?"

"It does sound queer," the bronze man admitted. "This man talks Sixteenth-Century English, but I do not know why or anything else about it. It is very strange. But you might get on our trail. Have you got a radio direction-finder handy?"

"Sure. There's one in a car downstairs."

"I will leave this transmitter turned on," Doc explained. "They may not notice it. I will also lay the microphone on the transmitter so it will pick up generator hum. You trace us with the direction-finder."

"Then what?"

"You might have to use your own judgment."

"On my way!" Monk said. Then as an afterthought he added. "How many of them Shakespeares is there?"

"Two men are in the van, but only one is a Shakespeare, as you term it. At least one or two more men were in the car that bumped my machine up into the van."

"As long as they ain't over a dozen," Monk said confidently, "I can handle 'em."

"Bring Ham."

"Oh—O. K.," Monk grumbled.

Doc switched off the receiver portion of the radio, so that static noises would not draw attention. Then he got out and leaned against the car to wait. All his men—he had five assistants—made it a practice to have instant two-way radio communication available at all possible times.

The bronze man had radios everywhere—in cars, planes, boats, apartments, and even portable short-range sets which could be carried around in pockets. Sometimes the devices were not used for weeks, and they began to seem like useless gimmicks. But when they were needed, it was usually no fooling.

Then the truck stopped. The back of the van opened. Two men with guns got in.

One was the wide man with the incredibly homely face and the imitation pearl tie pin. The other was bitter-looking Henry. Under their topcoats, both fellows wore breastplates of steel armor which looked rather ancient.

"Perchance thou can touch the roof!" suggested Henry gloomily.

Doc demonstrated that he could.

Henry walked around and handcuffed the bronze man. Henry's wide companion went over and peered under the dashboard of the car. He chuckled.

"Yep!" he said. "He's had the radio workin'!"

Henry asked, "You think, sire, perchance his friends may locate the transmitter with another device?"

"Good bet."

"Aye, then 'tis well," Henry said, wearing, however, the expression of a boy who had lately learned there was no Santa Claus.

Doc Savage said, "You knew that was on?" He pointed at the radio.

"Aye, we knew." Henry sighed. "We ourselves do have a short-wave radio. We heard thee converse with one addressed as Monk."

"You are leading Monk and Ham into a trap?" Doc demanded sharply.

"Aye."

Monk, Lieutenant Colonel Andrew Blodgett Mayfair, was a man who was easily satisfied; but nothing that Brigadier General Theodore Marley "Ham" Brooks did would ever satisfy him.

"Somethin' must be wrong with you!" Monk complained.

"Why?" Ham snapped.

"Well, you ain't drivin' in the center of the road for a change."

Ham, who was driving the big limousine, turned around to give the homely Monk a bilious eye. Ham was a lean-waisted man who was known in the higher spheres of civilization as the best-dressed man of the day. However, he was also a lawyer, and he had practiced putting a bilious eye on witnesses in court. He wielded a very bilious eye.

"One more crack out of you," Ham said, "and I'll tap you on top of that wart you call a head so hard that you'll think the eyelets in your shoes are windows!"

Monk ignored that. He gave attention to the little portable radio direction-finder which he was manipulating.

"Head more to the south," he ordered. Then he added, "I wonder if Doc could have gone wacky?"

"Wacky?"

"Well, that talk about people speakin' Sixteenth-Century English sounds wacky, don't it?"

"If it wasn't against my policy to agree with you," Ham muttered, "I'd say it was."

They crossed a bridge over the East River, followed boulevards, and passed beyond the suburbs of New York City. The car rocketed through a flat, sandy region of truck farms.

"The signal is gettin' louder," Monk announced. And later, he declared, "We're right on it! I can hear Doc's generator hum like nobody's business!"

The car passed a low rambling white house with green

shutters which sat in a nest of shrubbery. Monk swung the radio loop excitedly.

"They're there!" he barked.

Behind the low white house stood a white shed and a white barn, and they were also surrounded with brush.

"Regular jungle," Ham said.

"Doc said they bumped his car up in a big van, didn't he?" Monk asked.

"Yeah."

"The van is probably in the shed or the barn. We might as well drive right in, hadn't we?"

"That is as good a course as any," Ham said, "even if the idea was yours."

The aids drove up the road a bit, turned around and came back. They might be heading into plenty of trouble, but neither was much bothered. Without looking at all like a rolling fortress, the sedan had bulletproof glass, armor-plate steel sides and gasproof sealing.

And while the car did not look like an armory, compartments held machine-pistols, gas masks, smoke bombs, demolition bombs, and there was a tank slung under the chassis filled with a type of gas which would make a man unconscious whether he wore an ordinary gas mask or not. The stuff would get in through the skin pores.

Ham wheeled the sedan into the driveway.

Out of the shrubbery stepped four men wearing trim blue uniforms and shiny badges.

"Huh!" Monk exploded. "Cops!"

Chapter IV

PRINCE ALBERT

THE men in uniforms peered into the limousine, and one of them said, "Say, aren't you Monk and Ham, the two Doc Savage aids?"

The voice, heard through the armorplate steel and bullet-proof glass, was very faint. Monk lowered the window a trifle.

"That's right," he said. "We're Monk and Ham."

"Quite a coincidence," said the uniformed man.

Monk said, "How do you mean?"

"One of the neighbors around here called the police and said there were some queer-acting characters around here," the man in blue explained. "We came to investigate, and got here in time to catch them making a prisoner of Doc Savage."

"The dickens you did!" Monk said.

"Yep. They had worked the dangdest gag on him. Bumped his car up inside a big steel moving van."

"Is Doc all right?" Monk demanded anxiously.

"Sure."

"That's swell." Monk opened the car door. "What's it all about?"

"Why was Doc Savage grabbed, you mean?"

"Yeah. Why was he?"

"He says he don't know. We don't know, either. We can't make head or tail of it. They just up and grabbed him."

Monk muttered, "That's queer."

"You bet. It's the dangdest thing."

"Where are the birds who grabbed Doc? And where's Doc?"

"They're all in the house. You want to help us question the mugs who grabbed Doc?"

"I'll say I do!" Monk scrambled out of the limousine. "I'll bet I can make 'em talk. I'll take the arms and legs off 'em!"

13

MONK started for the house. Ham got out of the limousine and followed him. Habeas Corpus and Chemistry also got out of the car and joined the procession. Habeas Corpus was a runty-looking pig with long legs, enormous ears and a snout built for exploring. Chemistry was a remarkable-looking ape which bore an astounding resemblance to the homely chemist, Monk.

Fully fifteen men sprang up out of the shrubbery without the slightest warning. They fell upon Monk and Ham. Monk began to roar and bellow as he always did when he fought, but the noise did not help much. Within seconds, he and Ham were flat on their backs and ropes were being tied around their ankles and wrists.

The man who had been spokesman of the fake cops took off his uniform cap and blue coat. Both Monk and Ham were then fascinated with the fellow's width and his homeliness.

The wide man addressed one of his companions, a fellow who looked as if he was holding a bad oyster in his mouth.

"Henry," the wide man said, "we'll take them inside as soon as they are tied."

"Aye, sire," said the bilious-looking Henry.

"Where did the hog and the ape go, Henry?" the wide man asked.

"They ran away, sire," Henry explained.

"Then you had better take some of the boys and run after 'em."

"Aye," Henry said.

The wide man now turned to Monk and Ham and showed his teeth with a kind of grim cheerfulness.

"I'm the Prince," the wide man said.

Monk blinked. "Prince?"

"Prince Albert," the man said.

"Who do you think you're kiddin'?" Monk demanded.

"I'll bite," the man said. "Brother, when you hear me called anythin' but Prince Albert, I'm your genie."

"My what?"

"Genie. Came with Aladdin's lamp, remember? Just rub me and make a wish."

Monk and Ham exchanged speculative looks, wondering if their new acquaintance was touched in the head.

"Humph!" Monk said.

Prince Albert waved at Monk and Ham. "Take them inside," he said, "and give them the full benefit of our accommodations."

Monk and Ham were carried inside the house and placed in a room which had a low-beamed ceiling. Arrayed around the room were a number of remarkably heavy chairs.

Doc Savage was confined to one of these chairs by stout ankle-and-wrist manacles. The big bronze man looked at them and smiled slightly.

"A labyrinthine imbroglio, as Johnny would say," he remarked.

"That's probably it," Monk said. "The words sound like they would about fit."

Monk and Ham were now manacled to the large chairs. Monk lunged against the fastenings. He could take horseshoes in his two hands and change their shapes. However, the chair was too stout for him.

"Unusual chairs," Doc Savage commented.

Prince Albert waved at the chairs. "Part of our special preparations for you birds."

"Yeah?" Monk scowled.

Prince Albert grinned. "The welcomin' party of fake cops wasn't bad, either—or didn't you think so?"

"Humph!" Monk grunted. "What's the idea?"

"Wanted you out of the way."

Monk peered intently at the man who called himself Prince Albert. "Never saw you before. Never heard of you before, either."

"Have I claimed different?"

"What're you up to?"

"Probably more than you suspect, I hope."

Monk, scowling, said, "You haven't got all our crowd out of the way. There's three others left."

"I know." Prince Albert laughed. "Johnny Littlejohn, the archæologist, Long Tom Roberts, the electrical wizard, and Renny Renwick, the engineer. But they're in Europe."

Monk grimaced. "You're pretty well posted."

The other nodded.

"Considerin' that we're goin' up against Doc Savage," he said, "it would pay to be posted, don't you think?" He frowned at Doc Savage. "I must say that I'd feel better if he looked more worried."

AT this point, Henry came in from outdoors. Sweat had soaked his clothing, and he held a fist against the left side of his chest and panted heavily.

Prince Albert scowled. "Haven't you caught 'em?"

"Sire, they run like deer!"

"Get back out there," said Prince Albert, "and run like deer yourselves."

The sweating, panting Henry ran out grumbling.

Prince Albert now entered another room, where he changed clothes. He was very careful with the immaculate, expensively tailored garb which he had been wearing, but not so painstaking with what he put on. He donned a suit which looked as if it might have been taken off a not-too-self-respecting tramp.

He went back to the prisoners, seemed worried by Doc Savage's lack of visible concern, and entertained himself examining the labels in Ham's expensive clothing and wrinkling his homely nose scornfully.

"Tenth Avenue hand-me-down stuff," he sneered. "These sack-makers haven't any right to call themselves tailors."

This was probably the one remark that would drive Ham wild. Berate him, slander his character, libel his ancestors, besmirch his associates, and he no more than took offense. But saying a bad word about his clothes was like killing his kid brother.

Ham turned purple, tried to say several things, and succeeded in sounding like a dog caught under a fence.

Henry came back into the room. He was panting harder than ever, and had removed his shirt to sweat more freely.

By one ear, Henry carried Habeas Corpus, the pig.

He puffed, "A rabbit, sire—could'st run—no faster!"

Prince Albert scowled. "What about the ape?"

"Sire, the men have it up a tree."

PRINCE ALBERT walked over and peered at Habeas Corpus. He did not seem reassured.

"Better put that thing in a sack," he ordered. "I can turn it loose when I need to exhibit it as my pet."

This caused Monk to rear up in astonishment.

"Hey!" the homely chemist squawked. "You fixin' to pass as me?"

"Think I'll make it?" Prince Albert asked dryly.

Monk yelled, "What the blazes kind of game are you pullin'?"

"I'll bet you two bits," the homely man said, "that I get away with it."

"What," Monk howled, *"is this all about?"*

"Let's not be pikers," Prince Albert said. "Make it five dollars. What say? Five bucks I get away with being you."

Monk buzzed. He had to be very mad before he buzzed.

Doc Savage spoke. He used ancient Mayan, an almost unknown language which he and his men employed when it was better that bystanders should not understand.

"Take it easy," the bronze man advised. "As soon as he leaves, we'll start a little campaign of our own."

"Campaign?" Monk muttered.

"Let's hope that describes it."

Prince Albert scowled at them and said, "I don't know what you're sayin', but if you know what's good for you, don't pull any shenanigans."

"We wouldn't think of it," Monk said dryly.

Prince Albert snorted. Then he yelled, "Henry!"

"Aye." The pickled-looking Henry appeared.

"Henry, you take a car and drive to the submarine and see that it is ready for sea as soon as possible," Prince Albert ordered. "I think we've about got our business wound up, so we can vamoose."

"But the prisoners, sire?" Henry ventured.

"I'll leave 'em here under guard. You go to the submarine, Henry."

"Aye," Henry said.

Chapter V

GIRL IN ARMOR

Doc Savage's headquarters occupied the eighty-sixth floor of one of Manhattan's tallest buildings, and it was an enormous, modernistic Aladdin's cavern consisting of a reception room, a library containing one of the finest collections of scientific tomes in existence, and a laboratory holding instruments which scientists came from all over the world to observe.

There was a pneumatic tube running from the place to Doc Savage's boathouse and airplane hangar on the Hudson water front, and there was also a private high-speed elevator to the private garage in the basement of the skyscraper. However, ordinary visitors came up in the regular elevators.

Prince Albert came up in the ordinary way: in an elevator. He wore a large hat yanked down over his eyes, an enveloping yellow topcoat, and he carried a large traveling bag with holes punched in the end.

The door of Doc Savage's aërie was bulletproof steel painted bronze, with no knob or keyhole. The door was opened electromechanically by the effect of a radioactive material on an electric eye hidden in the wall.

The "keys" were small coin-shaped pieces of radioactive metal which Doc Savage and his men carried. When a "key" was brought near the electric eye, mechanism did the rest.

Prince Albert had taken Monk's "key," and he seemed to know how the door functioned, because he opened it and entered. Then he took off his hat and long coat and put them out of sight. His next operation was to close all doors and windows and select a brassie from a bag of golf clubs standing in a corner.

Opening his large traveling bag with care, he let the pig Habeas Corpus escape. When the shote showed inclination for hostilities, Prince Albert made a few warning passes with the brassie.

"You're a convenience around here, hog," he said. "And not an absolute essential. Just paste that on your snoot."

Habeas Corpus retreated to a corner, and the homely man picked up one of the several telephones which stood on the inlaid table that, with a huge safe, comprised the principal furniture of the reception room. He dialed a number.

"Hello!" He apparently recognized the voice which answered. "Put Henry on the wire."

There was a delay, and Prince Albert waited patiently.

Then Henry spoke sadly over the telephone.

"How now," Henry inquired, "has aught gone amiss?"

"Nope. So far, it's been slick as silk." Prince Albert chuckled. "How's the new sub comin'? Can we shove off by daylight?"

"They work frantically," Henry said gloomily.

"Hell, they've been workin' frantically all the time! Will they get done in time?"

"Perchance."

"There'd better not be any chance about it. I'm in Doc Savage's headquarters now. Some joint, too!" Prince Albert grinned widely. "I'm all set for the girl—when she shows up."

"Dost thee feel able to seize her alone?" Henry asked dubiously.

"Sure. She won't get away."

"Perchance it will cost us some millions of dollars if she does."

"To say nothin'," added Prince Albert, "of the hangin'-bee that would follow."

" 'Twould be firing squads," Henry said.

He did not sound as if he was trying to be funny.

That terminated the conversation. Prince Albert sat in a chair, parked his heels on the edge of the table, kept his brassie handy and a wary eye on Habeas Corpus, and waited something over two hours, after which knuckles gave the door a tapping. Prince Albert opened the door.

"Good evenin'," he said. "Somethin' we can do for you?"

THE girl said, "Forsooth, it may'st be thou——" She caught herself, changed to, "Brother, you said a mouthful!"

"Do come in," Prince Albert said.

The girl examined him. She was a long, corny girl with well-made rather than delicate features, a large and nice mouth, and an arrogant mass of cornsilk hair. She wasn't the kind of girl you thought of as cuddly.

Rather, you pictured her in a chorus line, or yelling her head off at the races, or balanced on an aquaplane behind a motor boat doing forty an hour. She was a nice athletic-looking girl. And she also looked like a girl who could take care of herself.

"What can I do for you, miss——"

"Miss China Janes," she said.

"Huh?" Prince Albert said, and looked as if he had been hit with a hammer.

"I know it's a funny name," China Janes said. "But usually it doesn't floor 'em."

Prince Albert tried to talk, but the best he could do was make two or three strange noises. He covered his vocal confusion by coughing behind a hairy hand.

"Somethin' in my throat," he explained. "I beg your pardon, Miss Janes. I am Lieutenant Colonel Andrew Blodgett Mayfair, called Monk by my friends. I hope you will call me Monk."

"I seem to have read somewhere," China Janes remarked, "that you were a fast worker."

Prince Albert looked as pleased as he could. He indicated the belligerent pig.

"This," he said, "is Habeas Corpus, my pet pig."

The girl examined the pig. "You two don't seem to be getting along together."

"Oh, we're havin' one of our tiffs."

Wearing a manufactured grin, Prince Albert led China Janes to a chair, seated her with a flourish, then planted himself opposite her.

"What," he asked, "may we do for you?"

"Nothing for me, I hope," the girl said. "But I've got a friend who thinks you can do plenty for her. From the way she talks, you'll be doing the rest of humanity quite a man-sized good turn at the same time."

"And who," Prince Albert asked, "is your friend in need?"

"Her Highness, the Duchess Portia Montanye-Norwich," China Janes replied.

Prince Albert tried not to look as relieved as he felt.

"Ah," he said, "royalty."

"Um-m. It depends on how you look at it." The girl leaned forward. "But look here. Portia sent me to get Doc Savage. The poor kid needs help bad. Is Doc here?"

Prince Albert, shaking his head regretfully, said, "Doc Savage is away on an important mission, and will not be available for a number of days."

"That," China Janes said, "is tough. From what I've read of Doc Savage, a screwy business like this is right up his alley."

"However," Prince Albert murmured, "I am a Doc Savage associate, and glad to be at your service."

The girl examined Prince Albert and frowned. She seemed apprehensive.

"If I hadn't heard so much about Doc Savage's outfit," she said, "I'd be doubtful. But I guess it's all right."

"Of course it is all right."

CHINA JANES leaned back.

"I'll go back to the beginning," she said. "When I first met the Duchess Portia Montanye-Norwich, she was plain Portia Bowen, and we both kicked a wicked heel in the same chorus. Portia and I got to be friends. We had something in common. We both liked to get out and do things. That was six years ago. That is, it was six years ago when Portia grabbed off her duke.

"Boy, was she lucky! The duke was rolling in shekels. He didn't know how much money he had. Portia took him back to England, and they lived in the family castle for two years; and then the duke was killed in a plane crack-up.

"Portia went haywire after that. She loved the guy, I guess. Anyway, she started flying to Cape Town and across oceans. Remember when she flew the Atlantic?"

Prince Albert admitted, "Seems I do recall such an event."

"She was a wow. And all through those years, I never saw her." China sighed. "Oh, we swapped a letter now and then. But two years ago, her letters stopped coming. She had disappeared. I never saw anything in the newspapers about it.

But my letters all came back. That happened for two years. Then this afternoon, she walked in on me."

"The duchess appeared this afternoon?"

"Maybe you'd call it materialized. Ghosts materialize, don't they?"

"Eh?"

"After you take a look at her, you'll understand. Plenty had happened to her. You could see that."

"Just what had occurred?"

"She didn't tell me."

"Heh!" Prince Albert looked relieved in spite of himself. "She didn't, eh?"

"Not a thing." China Janes leaned forward excitedly. "But you remember the submarine that blew up near Boston?"

"Hm-m. Yes, indeed."

"Remember that a yacht rescued a girl and brought her ashore, and she got away?"

"Well——"

"And the girl wore pieces of medieval armor?"

"Yes, I recall——"

"And she talked the kind of English they spoke four or five hundred years ago?"

"I read somethin' of the sort," Prince Albert admitted. "It sounded fantastic."

"You bet it did. And it's a lot more fantastic now that I know the girl was my old kicking mate, Portia."

"Goodness!" said Prince Albert.

"And she won't tell me a thing. Oh, she talks. But such talk!" China made a face. "She sounds like one of them Shakespeare plays. 'Forsooth' and 'thou' and 'thee' and that kind of stuff. Spills it with a straight face, too."

China Janes pounded both fists on the arms of the chair in which she sat. "I tell you, something has happened to that girl! Something that's done things to her mind! She keeps raving about a lot of people who need help."

PRINCE ALBERT stood up. He did his best to look like a deeply sympathetic man who intended to do something about this.

"What about these people who need help?"

"She won't go into details," China said.

"I shall speak to Duchess Portia Montanye-Norwich at once," Prince Albert said emphatically. "Where can I find her?"

China said, "I'll take you there."

The man made a business of considering that, then shook his head pleasantly.

"It would be better," he said, "if you told me where she can be found. I will send some of Doc Savage's men after her."

"But——"

"You may be in danger," Prince Albert interrupted. "If I were you, I would stay here until we find out what this is about. You said the duchess was scared, didn't you? If she is scared, obviously there is danger."

China thought that over.

"O. K.," she said. "The duchess—Portia—is at my apartment. 476 North Avenue, Apartment 12."

Prince Albert went to the telephone, dialed a number, and said, "I've got the dame located." He gave the address China Janes had just furnished. "Get her out of there and where she can't talk."

Prince Albert then listened a moment.

"Yeah," he told the party at the other end of the wire, "I've got another dame here that we'll have to keep quiet, too."

He put down the phone, turned, took a gun out of his coat pocket, pointed it at China Janes.

"Tough break, kid," Prince Albert said. "I'm afraid you're goin' to be out of circulation from now on."

China Janes's eyes got very wide. She seemed to try to stand on tiptoes.

"I don't—what——"

"Turn around!" the man said.

Something in Prince Albert's eyes made the girl scream. She screamed as if trying to get out every bit of noise possible.

"My understandin'," the man said, "is that this place is soundproof." His voice went guttural. *"Turn around!"*

China Janes hesitated, her teeth nearly making holes in her lips. Very slowly, she wheeled around and put her back to the man.

Prince Albert got a long needle out of his clothing and took a step toward the girl.

Then he jumped as high into the air as he could. He also screamed as loud as he could.

Just before Prince Albert jumped, a swarm of blue sparks buzzed up around his feet. After he came back to the floor, the sparks appeared again, sizzling, snapping.

Chapter VI

LOST RACES

PRINCE ALBERT had presence of mind. Electricity was smashing through his body, convulsing his muscles and swiping colored lights across his eyes. But he still controlled himself enough to look down, realize the carpet had become electrified, twist wildly out of his raincoat and fling it to the floor. There was enough rubber in the coat to make an insulator. When he jumped upon it, no more sparks flew.

The girl stood wide-eyed. There was no electric fire around her feet.

Prince Albert had dropped his gun. Trying to get it, he sprang out on the carpet. Sparks grew around his feet like hot blue animals snarling and gnashing.

When he took hold of his gun, he got as much blue electric fire as gun. He could not hold the weapon. He screamed in spite of himself. He tried again. He could not make his fingers take the gun.

Prince Albert gave it up, did a kangaroo jump to the insulating raincoat. Agony was turning his face the purple of a man choking. Bawling noises he made were probably his best at swearing.

From the coat, he sprang to the door. With both hands, he clutched the knob. But he let go of the knob instantly, peered at his hands. He saw pricked spots, as if there had been a thorn or two on the doorknob.

Prince Albert got his face close enough to the doorknob to see the little steel needles which had projected and stung him, and he could also see that they were hollow, and that drops of a syrupy, yellow substance had oozed from the steel fangs.

He frog-jumped backward from the door, making mewing noises of agitation, and hit the library door. It was locked.

25

The electricity on the rug—it was obvious now that wires were cleverly woven into the rug design to carry high-frequency current—shook him with paralytic violence. Back to the coat, he floundered.

Deadness was coming into his hands, crawling up his arms. He'd soon be helpless. He realized that.

Trade threat on the girl's life for his release? Who was there to trade with? There might be nobody; all this could be a wholly mechanical burglar trap.

Kill the girl? That had been orders, as a last resort.

Prince Albert got his knife out of his clothing and made for the girl—took two steps and mashed his out-thrust face against something hard and cold. Glass. Incredibly transparent plate.

He struck at it, hit it with his shoulder and all his weight. The stuff had come down from the ceiling. His own yelling must have covered the sound it made.

Because of the glass, he could not reach the girl.

Prince Albert was trapped! Certainty of that closed in on him like ice. He couldn't escape. There was nothing, then, but do what they were supposed to do when about to be taken. Every man of his gang carried the pills. The pills were issued fresh every two weeks.

He snatched the stick pin out of his necktie, twisted out the large, yellowish, cheap-looking artificial pearl with his teeth, crushed it and swallowed it.

Prince Albert was still swallowing parts of the pill when the bronze man came in through the library door.

Doc Savage had been taken by surprise to a certain extent—he had not expected the stick pin to turn out to be some kind of dose—and the bronze man was a bit disconcerted.

One of the main purposes of his lifetime of scientific training had been to equip his mind to foresee every contingency in any given situation. It was very necessary that his mind should be keen enough to overlook no bets at all. Otherwise, he could become a remarkably poor insurance risk. And just now he had overlooked a bet: the pearl-pill.

High-voltage, high-frequency current was out of the cleverly wired rug. Doc had thrown a switch. With faint-whispering sounds of electric motors, the bulletproof glass emergency partitions were lifted into the ceiling.

Doc Savage reached the man who called himself Prince Albert. The fellow evidently had confidence in his own strength, for he stepped in swinging. He swung four times, blows almost too fast for the eye. He made a perfect score. All misses. His eyes popped.

He said, *"Uhn!"* foolishly after the last miss.

Prince Albert was seeing dazzling speed such as he would not have believed human muscles could contrive. He tried a fifth blow. At the bronze man's midriff, this time.

But the fist went through space where the target had been. And in return, he was knocked down. After that, bronze hands handled him as if he had no strength whatever.

Doc Savage clamped Prince Albert down, got the fellow's jaws distended with pressure, yanked the man's belt off, and tried, by forcing the end of the belt down the fellow's throat, to force him to bring up the pills he had swallowed. That didn't work.

Carrying the man into the laboratory, Doc used a stomach pump. That took time. Enough time so that the man had become unconscious from the effects of the pill.

In the laboratory was a device for making quick chemical analysis by spectrascopic methods. The pill, this contrivance showed, contained ingredients which gave the nervous system such a shock that complete unconsciousness for days was certain.

Prince Albert was not likely to die. He was not likely to answer questions for some time, either.

Doc Savage walked into the reception room. The girl was fooling around with the outer door, trying to get it open.

"The excitement is probably over for the time being," the bronze man said. "So you might as well remain."

China Janes stared at him. She was noticeably impressed. Women usually were.

"You," she said, "are Doc Savage."

"Right."

"Who was that other man?"

"He wasn't Monk," Doc said quietly. "He called himself Prince Albert, and he and a number of other men went to a great deal of trouble to seize myself and Monk and Ham. The other men, incidentally, speak English after the manner of the day of Shakespeare."

China looked startled. "Perchance thou dost mean they speak after this fashion—that the kind of lingo they sling?"

"Exactly."

"The Duchess Portia Montanye-Norwich," China said, "talks like that."

"An interesting point."

"But that mug—that Prince Albert—he talked the regular way."

"Also interesting," Doc admitted. "By the way, I overheard all you told him. Did you leave out anything?"

"Not a thing. Told him all I knew."

"Portia mentioned people in need of help, you said."

"But that's all she did mention. I guess whoever is in trouble is pretty bad off." China frowned. "What is this crazy thing all about?"

"That," Doc said, "is what interests us. We have not the slightest idea, so far."

China took in a shaky breath. "Portia—the duchess—sure handed me something, didn't she?"

"She did. Suppose we go ask her about that, and other things?"

"Suits me."

Doc and the girl took the speed elevator to the street. Having come down eighty-six floors at practically free-falling speed, China Janes struggled with her breathing and her composure. The dark sedan which the bronze man drove rolled several blocks before she got organized.

"You say some men seized you?" she said. "When was that?"

"To-day."

"But—you're here now! You escaped?"

"Monk, Ham and myself," Doc explained, "carry small containers of an odorless and colorless gas which causes almost immediate unconsciousness without doing much harm. We used it on our guards and escaped."

"Didn't they search you?"

"They neglected to take the heels off our shoes."

"Oh!"

Doc Savage switched on a short-wave radio "transceiver," and said into the microphone, "Monk!"

"Yeah, Doc?" Monk's squeaky voice responded.

"Questioned any of those men yet?"

"Sure. But so far we've got what the little boy shot at. Boy, they won't talk like Shakespeare or any other way!"

"We will try truth serum."

"That may do it. Where are you now, Doc?"

"Going after the other girl."

"Girl? What girl?"

Tension jumped across the bronze man's features. "Monk! Didn't Prince Albert call you, and didn't you make one of the prisoners answer, and Prince Albert told him where to find the Duchess Portia Montanye-Norwich?"

"Nothing like that happened, Doc."

"Then there must be two gangs in New York!"

"Two gangs of who?"

"These fellows speaking Sixteenth-Century English. Prince Albert evidently called the second gang."

"This is gettin' complicated," Monk complained. "Doc, have you been able to figure this mess out?"

The fact that the bronze man did not answer was not unusual. Those associated with him were accustomed to the habit. His silence usually came when he was unsure, or did not wish to commit himself. When asked his opinion of what a puzzling chain of events meant, he frequently failed to answer.

Doc touched a button, and a siren began whining under the car hood, and red police lights glowed front and rear. Traffic cops blew whistles; motorists angled toward curbs and stopped, and there was room for speed. The speedometer needle started a march for the other side of the dial.

The velocity with which they whipped around street cars made China Janes take several bites at the ends of her fingers. She fell to staring at the floor because it was easier on her nerves.

"You think Portia may be in danger?" she asked.

"Indications point that way."

The car slowed, skidding a little, arched around a corner, then took more speed with an abruptness that dragged them back against the cushions.

China said, "Portia was on that submarine."

"You sure?" Dock asked.

"She said so. And she's wearing part of a chain-mail armor. Remember the newspapers said something about the armor?"

THE bronze man cut the siren, began to reduce speed. Traffic closed in around the machine, and they made no more commotion than other motorists.

"There," China said, "is where I live."

The building was tall, modern and brick, with many wide windows and an awning out in front, under which stood a doorman in uniform. A good class of apartment house.

The car drifted up and touched its running board to the curb. Doc Savage said, "You'd better stick here."

"But——"

"The doors lock. The body is armorplate, the windows bulletproof. The car's interior is gas-tight."

"Since there's no fort handy," China said, "the car suits me." She settled back. "Apartment 12."

Doc Savage got out and went to the doorman. "Anything strange happened around here?" he asked.

The doorman had a remarkably red face, pale-blue eyes and a long blond mustache. The utter blue of his eyes made them seem blank.

"Doc Savage?" he asked.

Doc did not quite show surprise. "Yes."

The doorman said, "I have a message for you."

He reached under the tails of his uniform coat and took out a pistol which was a flintlock weapon and must have been in excess of two hundred years old.

"Methinks thou best stand still," he said.

When Doc Savage reached for him, the man did not hesitate about pulling the trigger.

Chapter VII

MISSING DUCHESS

THE old horse pistol made enough smoke for a camp fire and enough noise for an earthquake, and it coughed out a ball as large as the head of a sparrow.

The slug hit Doc Savage in the chest, rooted through coat, vest, shirt, and slammed up against the metallic alloy-mesh bulletproof undergarment which he had been forced, because of perpetual danger, to wear for years.

Shock drove air out of the bronze man's lungs. He coughed, got it back in. Then he grasped the man, clamped him close with one arm and took hold of the back of the fellow's neck and put pressure on neck nerve centers. The man did some extra-size kicking. Then he went rope slack. He would probably be out for an hour or more.

China Janes was getting out of the car.

Doc said, "Get back in there!"

"This means," the girl cried, "that they're already here!"

"Get back in the car," Doc said.

"Are you hurt?"

"No," Doc said.

The girl ducked back in the car. Doc Savage ran to the machine, and dumped the prisoner into the rear seat. The fellow slumped against the girl.

"Be back soon," Doc Savage said. "In case I'm not, take this fellow to the police."

China peered at the captive. "Don't I get a monkey wrench or something? Suppose he wakes up?"

Doc Savage left her to worry about that and went into the apartment house.

The genuine doorman and the elevator boy were lying in a small cubby used for storing mops and buckets. They were bound and gagged. The bronze man freed them, put half a dozen quick questions, and learned that about all they knew was that they had stood unsuspecting while strangers approached them, had been astounded when the strangers presented the business ends of large flintlock pistols, and had prudently thought it better not to resist.

Both had noticed that their captors spoke somewhat quaint English. More than that, they did not know. Miss China Janes—yes, they knew her. The Duchess Portia Montanye-Norwich—was she the strange-looking girl who was visiting China? No, they didn't know anything about her. No, the raiders hadn't asked about her.

They must have known all about her, however. She was gone when Doc Savage went upstairs. She might have been gone about fifteen minutes. At least, some one had jerked the cord of an electric clock out of the light socket that long ago.

There was not much doubt but that the cord had been jerked during the course of a fight. There were upset chairs, a shattered vase, and furniture pushed askew.

Doc Savage went down to his car.

"Your duchess," he said, "seems to be a certain percentage of wildcat."

China dampened her lips. "They got Portia?"

"Yes."

"When?"

"Not very long ago," Doc Savage said. "Can you drive?"

"If you don't mind taking chances."

"Head back for my headquarters." Doc Savage turned on the siren, added, "About all you have to do is keep in the middle of the street."

China drove. She had told the truth about her driving being all right if you didn't mind taking chances.

DOC SAVAGE turned on the radio transmitter-receiver, then turned knobs and took it off the wave length employed by himself and his men. He shifted to the frequency used by the navy. He contacted a navy shore station, and was, in turn, put through to an admiral.

"It has occurred to me," the bronze man explained, "that there might be interesting angles to the sinking of that submarine *Swordfish* near Boston."

"Who is this?"

Doc Savage made his identity known. The admiral seemed pleased.

"We thought of you," the admiral said.

"Thought of me?"

"Sure. This submarine business needs the kind of touch you've got."

"Maybe it would help," Doc said, "if you explained about the submarine."

"Can you speak Arabic?"

"Yes," Doc said.

The admiral said, "Swell. I worked in Arabia long enough to learn the language, and I'll use it to explain about that submarine. Chances nobody who overhears will understand."

He went on talking and told Doc Savage that the U. S. navy had no idea who owned the submarine or what had caused it to sink. However, he stated, the U. S. navy was sure it hadn't lost any submarines.

And he added that, although officially the affair was being dropped to avoid an international incident, nevertheless navy officials would much like to question the mysterious girl wearing ancient armor who had been saved from the sub.

"Now," the admiral ended, "it's your turn. What got you into this crazy thing?"

Doc Savage said, "The rather interesting angles."

"You're not kidding me," the admiral said. "But don't be explicit if you don't want to."

"Thanks," Doc said.

"To satisfy my own curiosity, though, I'd like to know what you finally find out about it."

"That is a promise," Doc said.

The admiral gave a disgusted snort. "Find out why the girl wore armor. The blasted army is already beginning to kid us about any girl on one of our boats needing a suit of armor."

That was about the extent of the conversation.

Climbing back into the rear seat of the car Doc Savage went to work on the spinal nerve centers of the prisoner, and by massage and realigning of spinal vertebræ, relieved the congestion which was keeping the man helpless. The fellow began to groan and roll his eyes.

Doc said, "That was an American-built submarine which sank off Boston."

The captive must have understood, but he did not say anything.

"Descriptions of the sub," Doc continued, "were too accurate to be mistaken. The submarine which blew up was named the *Swordfish,* and it was identical with the U. S. navy submarine named *Swordfish.* The *Swordfish* design is distinctive. There were two *Swordfishes.* Yet there is not supposed to be.

"No other nation has a *Swordfish* type boat, nor one that could be mistaken for a *Swordfish.* No other sub, for instance, has a streamlined forward superstructure housing a seaplane."

The captive's red face grew a little redder. All of him looked as if it had been exposed to a great deal of sea weather. He was stubbornly silent.

"Do you know what truth serum is?" Doc asked.

"Faith, do'st thee think to frighten me?" the prisoner asked quietly enough.

China Janes, driving with concentration, took a corner, then threw a remark over her shoulder.

"Another thee-and-thou guy," she said.

Doc Savage took hold of the prisoner, and the man fought until Doc crowded him down on the floorboards and got the fellow's hands and feet bound and a wad of cloth between his teeth.

Then the bronze man took the steering wheel and drove to his private garage in the skyscraper's basement. Doc and the girl rode the private speed elevator upstairs, taking the prisoner.

When they came near the hall door of the bronze man's headquarters, the prisoner suddenly kicked, made animal noises. Doc studied the captive. He took another step toward the door. The prisoner came as near having a fit as he could, bound as he was.

Doc Savage glanced at China. "You had better go back."

The girl looked blank. "Why?"

INSTEAD of answering her, the bronze man stacked the captive in a corner, then took the girl's elbow and steered her inside the speed elevator, shut her up inside the cage, then pressed an external control button which sent the cage plummeting down.

Doc ignored the office door, went on down the corridor, and stopped close to an apparently blank wall. Here he went through what would have been an insane procedure, had it not been for a mechanism concealed inside the wall. The contraption inside the wall could best be described as a lock worked by a combination of sounds—finger tappings in this case.

The bronze man tapped the combination, carefully counting out the fractional-second timing. A sensitive amplifier, a relay and an electric motor did the rest, and a panel opened.

Without hesitating, Doc stepped through into a passage which was narrow because it occupied space between two false walls. It served the double purpose of a secret passage in or out of headquarters, and storage for stuff which the bronze man wished to keep out of sight. Doc got into the laboratory through another secret panel.

Laboratory, library and reception room were empty of human presence. The man who called himself Prince Albert was gone. And so was Habeas Corpus.

The pile of tinned trinitrotoluene against the headquarters door probably contained over a hundred quarts—not enough to blow the city off the map, but enough to make a decided impression on several square blocks.

The stuff was hooked to an electrical detonator which would have been set off had Doc opened the door.

Doc Savage disconnected the detonator and put it to one side. Then he moved the T. N. T. After that, he went out and put a metallic finger on a button which brought the speed elevator back.

China had evidently been trying to get out of the cage. However, it locked automatically when the external control buttons were used. She was a trifle discomfited.

"You might," she snapped, "give a girl some idea of what you intend doing next!"

Doc Savage looked amiable, but did not answer. One of the earlier bits of knowledge he had acquired was that the less conversation you had with an aggravated woman, the less your grief. He hauled the captive into the reception room, and China followed.

China said, "Mister, I'm getting darned tired of unexpected things happening!"

Still looking amiable, Doc Savage went to the radio, warmed the tubes, then said, "Monk!" into the microphone.

A minute later, he said, "Monk!" again. In the next two minutes, he asked the microphone for Monk or Ham almost a dozen times. And by then his metallic features had stopped trying to be amiable. The weird effect of motion in his flake gold eyes had become more pronounced.

To China, the bronze man said, "It might be the best idea for you to stick with me. These men may be convinced you know enough about them to be dangerous. They cannot be sure how much the Duchess Portia told you about them."

China frowned. "You think it'd be dangerous for me to walk around loose, eh?"

"Conceivably."

"From what I've seen," China said, "being around you doesn't make anybody a good insurance risk. But if you say so, I'm game. Where do we go first?"

"To see what has happened to Monk and Ham," Doc said.

He sounded concerned.

Doc Savage took twenty minutes for the trip to the Long Island farmhouse where he had left Monk and Ham, the distance being nearly that many miles. The fake doorman bounced around a good deal in the back seat during the trip.

The farmhouse, when they pulled up to it, had a deserted look.

Doc said, "You stay in the car."

"Don't worry," China retorted, "I appreciate this car. Nice and bulletproof, you know."

Doc put an electrical-listening device against the farmhouse door before he went in. The listener was a combination of velocity mike and amplifier, and could make a fly walking on velvet sound like an elephant in a jungle. Out of the house came complete silence, and he went in.

In the house there were fight signs: upset chairs, scuffed places on the floor, a chair leg with traces of somebody's hair sticking to it. Enough glass was missing from one window to make it look as if some one had jumped out of it. Only enough blood had been spilled to make spots. The house was as empty as the listener-amplifier device had indicated.

China, too curious to remain in the car any longer, entered. She peered about doubtfully, kicked an overturned chair, poked into closets, straightened a picture, and finally noticed that she had stepped on fine particles of glass.

She indicated the glass. "Somebody broke a light bulb."

"Anæsthetic grenades we used to overcome the guards earlier," the bronze man explained.

"Oh, I remember. That was when Prince Albert thought he had left you out here, a prisoner." She eyed the glass particles.

Doc Savage appeared not to hear.

"O. K. Don't answer me, then," China said. "Let's change the subject. What are you going to do about your missing friends?"

Instead of replying to that, the bronze man went outside and made several circles of the farmhouse, scrutinizing the ground closely. Then he searched the outbuildings. He did a very thorough job of this search, leading China to make a remark.

"There's a flyspeck you missed over here," she said.

By the time he ended his search, Doc Savage had concluded that the strange gang who talked ancient English vernacular, had been around the place only a day or two. And previous to their arrival, the farm had evidently been idle for months. He did not comment on this. His silence began to irritate China.

"You put out a lot of information, don't you?" she complained.

Doc Savage went into the house, got on the telephone and called the information girl at the telephone office and got a list of the real estate agents in the neighborhood.

He did not write down the names and telephone numbers —there was no need of that, with the memory he had developed. One of his memory exercises was to glance at an assortment of figures, then turn around and write them on a blackboard. It was not extraordinary for him to retain a hundred digits in his mind.

Doc telephoned real estate agents until he found the one

that had rented this old farm. It had been rented three days ago, cash in advance. The agent, describing the man who had rented the place, described Prince Albert.

"You're making headway fast," China said.

Chapter VIII

IRON SHARKS

Doc SAVAGE was a product of a deliberate scientific plan; he was the result of what could happen when physical instructors, psychologists and scientists all coöperated. The scientists and the others had assumed charge of Doc at childhood, and had taken turns in his training.

The bronze man had been in their hands almost continuously. His training should have made him a kind of superhuman scientific product. It should have made him a machine. It should have taken the human qualities out of him.

In one sense, all Doc Savage's training had been a flop: He still had his emotions. The things that pleased or excited other men pleased or excited him. Some of the scientists had tried to remove that, believing that a man being trained for his unusual profession should not have ordinary emotions. They would be a handicap.

For instance, Doc Savage could get just as scared as anybody. And as worried. Still, his past training had done one thing: it had fixed him up with a poker face, and he could, under almost any circumstances, show no emotion whatever.

China's repeated remarks about his lack of progress was sandpapering his nerves pretty raw.

"You," China said, "remind me of a rooster trying to scratch up a worm in a concrete street."

Doc Savage's mouth tightened, but he managed to hold onto himself.

"While you're fiddling," China continued, "these queer fellows who talk Old English are probably putting your friends Monk and Ham into sacks, tying weights to the sacks, and throwing the sacks into the river."

Doc's grip on his temper slipped. For the first time in his life, he told a lady off.

"Shut up!" he said loudly. "And sit down!"

China gazed at him in wide-eyed wonder. She righted an overturned chair and sat down on it.

"I actually believe," she gasped, "that you're almost human!"

Doc Savage did not wish to delve into any discussion to prove he was human. It wasn't important, as long as the young lady kept still.

The bronze man went back to the car and hauled out his prisoner, the fellow who had played doorman, and straightened him out on the farm floor. The captive lay loose, his eyes closed. It appeared that he had passed out again.

"I'll put him on the bed," Doc explained. "Then we will work on him and see how much truth we can get."

Doc Savage picked the man up in his arms, and carried him, somewhat as a father carries a baby, toward another room. They never made it to the room, however.

With convulsive speed, the prisoner jammed a hand into Doc Savage's pocket. The hand came out with the old horse pistol which Doc had taken from him earlier. The man pointed this monstrosity among firearms at Doc Savage.

"Thee will lower me gently!" he snarled.

After Doc lowered him gently, the man got to his feet. He included China in the menace of his gun.

"Thee"—he pointed the gun at the girl—"and thou, will betake theeselves to ye four-wheeled cart which dost run with noise."

They betook themselves outside and got in Doc's car, which was presumably what the man meant by "ye four-wheeled cart which dost run with noise." The man put them in the front seat. He got in the back.

"Now," the man said, "ye will go whence I tell ye."

Doc Savage drove out of the farmyard, and following the man's directions, turned left. Doc's features were inscrutable.

China leaned back on the cushions and shivered. The look she gave the bronze man was not approving.

"Thou," she snapped, "hast got us in a nice pickle!"

Doc Savage paid attention to his driving. He did not tell the girl that the horse pistol was not loaded, and that he had deliberately let the man grab the weapon; that he hoped the fellow would lead them somewhere, where they could escape, once they got there. There was no convenient way he could give China all this information, anyhow.

THEY passed a number of truck farms, then began to go past the small bungalows on the outskirts of the city. The herdsman in the back seat directed them to turn left again. Thereafter, Doc Savage began to suspect that they were headed for the water front district of Brooklyn.

China touched Doc Savage's arm.

"I'm sorry," she said, "that I made the crack about the pickle. I make cracks. It's a habit. You better overlook it."

"Forget it," Doc said.

China shivered again. "The heck I'll forget it. My old friend Portia swims ashore from a mysterious submarine that blew up, and she wants to talk to you; then a funny gang of ancient Englishmen grab her, and you, and me, and your two friends, all to hush the thing up. Forget it? Not as long as I live, I won't! It's too cockeyed!"

They came to a rough street, and Doc Savage drove on the street car tracks, where it was smoother.

"Everything may come out all right," he said.

"All right for who?" China asked grimly. "Two to one this bozo is taking us to more bozos just like him. Do you know what they'll do to us? If you don't, I do. They'll put us in those sacks I was telling you about."

The street got smooth again, and Doc steered the automobile off the street car tracks.

China sighed and ran her fingers through her honey-colored hair. "I hate being puzzled," she complained. "If it's the last thing that happens, I hope I learn what this is about. I'd hate to die puzzled."

One of the banes of any man's existence was a young woman who talked too much. Doc restrained himself from telling her so.

China seemed to be doing some thinking. As a result of this, she put her jaw up emphatically.

"Whatever happens," she said, "I'm going down fighting. When the funeral is over, they'll know they buried somebody."

It occurred to Doc Savage that, while the young lady did

have come aggravating traits, she did undoubtedly have a pleasant supply of courage.

IT developed that their captor knew where he was going. He directed them to an enormous solid wooden gate in a very high and very grimy brick wall near the water front. A sign along the top of this wall said:

MODERN MARINE CONSTRUCTION CO.

A gatekeeper opened the gate, then came forward to investigate the car. The gatekeeper had a thumb hooked in his belt, and just below this thumb swung a large military-looking automatic pistol in a holster.

The armed flunky looked in at China and Doc Savage, and seemed unimpressed. But when he glanced at the man sitting in the rear seat holding the horse pistol, he was much impressed.

"Great snakes!" he exploded.

"Pass us, vassal!" ordered the man with the horse pistol.

They were passed, and Doc followed directions and drove between large buildings, huge piles of steel plates, steel pipes, and steel girders. They passed under huge traveling cranes and circled tall derricks. They were deafened by the *rat-tat-tat* of riveting machines, and welding arcs threw blue-white light into the car.

"I think," China said, "that this is a—a——"

"Shipyard?"

"That's it. A place where they build ships."

Doc Savage adjusted the rear-view mirror to get a look at their shepherd. The fellow was holding the horse pistol in plain sight of any one who cared to look. Several persons in the shipyard must have seen the gun, but none of them did anything about it.

China decided to see what she could do to spur their chivalry.

"Help!" she screamed suddenly and piercingly. "Help! Murder! Get me out of here!"

At least a dozen men heard her shriek. They stopped working and looked at the car.

"Help!" China screeched, putting plenty of terror into it. "This man is going to kill us!"

The men who had stopped working went back to work as if nothing out of the ordinary had happened.

China sank back on the seat and shook.

"What—what kind of place is this?" she asked wildly.

"An unusual place, I should say," Doc Savage admitted.

"But—but—" China swallowed several times. "But—it's in Brooklyn! Right here in New York City. It's in—well, in Brooklyn!"

Under the circumstances, it did not make much difference whether it was in Brooklyn or where it was. Being in Brooklyn only made it a trifle more fantastic.

"Ho!" said the man in the back seat. "Stop, prithee!"

Doc Savage halted the car.

"Look!" China gasped. "A whole litter of submarines!"

Chapter IX

THE BREAKS

IT was apparent that while the shipyard might build other things, its main output was submarines. The iron fish lay in a row, four of them, side by side. The nearest was nearly done; the next had only half its hull plates; the third had no plates at all, and the fourth was not much more than a keel. The subs were being built on cradles which could be rolled down tracks into the water.

"Submarines!" China said. She looked at Doc Savage. "They should suggest something, but they don't."

The submarines were on the right. On the left stood the granddaddy of all boathouses. It lacked the height of the dirigible hangar at Lakehurst, but it appeared to have almost as much floor space. It was of brick, and had no windows. There were doors, however.

A door opened. Doc drove inside, as he was commanded. While several men were closing the door behind the car, he leaned out to look around.

Except for one thing, there was nothing particularly remarkable about the inside of the big boathouse. The one remarkable thing was the fact that a swarm of men seemed to be working at frantic speed putting a submarine together.

All the parts of this submarine seemed to be ready-made. Plates were the exact size, rivet holes were drilled, and everything was prepared for quick assembling.

It seemed a rather unusual way to build a submarine. And this sub appeared an exact twin of one that was being built outdoors.

"Here comes our old friend," China said grimly.

Doc had seen him. It was Prince Albert, and he was in a wheel chair. A laprobe was bundled around him to his chin, and he looked as if he was still very ill from the pill he had swallowed. He could, it seemed, barely wriggle his fingers and whisper, but this was enough to allow him to issue orders.

He issued some, and an astounding number of guns appeared in the hands of the men in the boathouse as they surrounded the car. Henry strolled sadly out of the belligerent mob, and opened the car door.

"Wouldst get out?" Henry asked.

Doc got out peaceably.

"And thee, as well," Henry told China.

The young woman also got out, but not peaceably. She stared about as if looking for some one to bite.

"I'm about ready," she said, "to do something desperate."

Doc Savage leaned close to her ear and whispered, "Take a deep breath, then hold it."

The girl had enough presence of mind not to show surprise, and she started drawing in her breath.

At that moment, there began climbing out of the submarine a group of men who were clad in what could pass for the very modern ski suits which girls wear, providing the suits were equipped with hoods of flexible, transparent stuff that looked like Cellophane. They carried rifles.

"Never mind holding your breath," Doc said. He sounded faintly disgusted.

China frowned. "First hold my breath, then don't." She made an angry shape with her rather attractive mouth. "I wonder who's slightly wacky around here?"

Doc Savage did not explain that he had been about to use his anæsthetic bombs—effects of which they could escape by holding their breath—but that the appearance of the group of men wearing gasproof suits had made that plan useless.

The bronze man began to have a vague suspicion that getting out of here might be quite a considerable job.

Doc and China were seized. Almost as many men got hold of them as could lay hands on them.

Prince Albert ordered his chair wheeled close, then said, "Give the girl a bathin' suit and put her in one of those big boxes, and give her five minutes to come out with the bathin' suit on."

China snapped, "If you think I'm taking your orders, you're crazy!"

"Maybe," Prince Albert said, "you'd like us to search you instead?"

China subsided, took the bathing suit they threw her, and got into a huge box which lay on its side with the open part toward the wall.

Prince Albert pointed at Doc Savage and said, "Frisk him, boys. I understand he wears a vest full of gadgets. Get that."

The men stripped the bronze man of coat, vest, shirt, and removed the alloy-mesh bulletproof vest which he wore. Then they went through his pockets.

They did a thorough job with their search, prying off his shoe heels and slapping under his arms and along the insides of his legs for any kind of weapon that might have been fastened there with adhesive tape. After that Doc received all his clothes back—minus his carry-all vest.

"Now," Prince Albert said, "let's see you get away."

China came out of her box, her very cute figure attired in a bathing suit which left absolutely no doubt about a number of things, including the fact that she could not possibly have concealed weapons. She had enough of effect to cause several moments of silent, profound admiration, which she didn't appreciate.

"Monkeys," she said, "seem to take to limbs."

Prince Albert mustered enough life to grasp the arms of his wheel chair and roll himself over to the girl. The effort so exhausted him that he glared at Doc Savage.

"Your fault I'm in this fix!" he complained. "If you hadn't been about to question me, I wouldn't have had to take that stuff to knock me out."

China told Prince Albert, "And if you hadn't been making trouble for people, you wouldn't have been in Doc Savage's office in the first place."

The incredibly homely fellow frowned at her.

"How," he asked China, "would you like to be a lady's maid?"

"I wouldn't like it," China said promptly.

"That's too bad," Prince Albert retorted, "because that's what you're goin' to be. Portia isn't satisfied. She needs someone——"

"I wouldn't think," China interrupted, "that she'd be satisfied around cutthroats. Portia has better taste."

"She needs a lady's maid," continued Prince Albert, ignoring the interruption, "and you're it. Old friend of hers, aren't you? That's swell. Take her away, boys."

Considerably over half the men shouted, "Yea, sire!" and attempted to appropriate the escort job; Prince Albert did some feeble, but violent swearing before he got it straightened out. Then Prince Albert leveled a finger at Doc Savage.

"We may need an out!" Prince Albert said dramatically.

"A what?" Doc inquired.

"Out. We've had to stir up things. Had to seize that girl. Had some trouble with you. The police are probably lookin' for us. If they find us, we'll need the out."

Doc asked, "Just what do you mean by an out?"

"You've got a lot of influence with the police."

"And so?"

"And so if you told 'em you had investigated us, and we were O. K., the cops would let us alone."

Doc Savage asked dryly, "And you think I would mislead the police?"

"I know you would," Prince Albert said with certainty. "We've got ways of makin' you."

This concluded that part of the conversation. Prince Albert issued orders, and a number of men fell upon Doc Savage. He did not resist them. The men led him up a long flight of movable steps to the deck of the submarine, thence down into the innards of the submersible. A door was unlocked. Doc was propelled through the door into intense darkness.

WITH great promptness, a voice said, "You take that side, Ham. I'll take this side." The voice was small and squeaky.

A deeper voice, an orator's voice, said, "We'll feel him over, Monk, and if he don't feel right, we'll let him have it."

Doc Savage said, "Let who have it?"

"Doc!" Monk squeaked.

"Of all people!" Ham whooped.

"Monk! Ham!" Doc Savage exclaimed. "Are you all right?"

It was obvious they were. They sounded too enthusiastic to be otherwise.

"Doc," Monk said, "don't tell me you're a prisoner, too? We were just telling each other how lucky it was you weren't in here. We figured one of 'em had come in to talk to us, and we were gonna give 'im the works."

Doc Savage asked, "What have you learned?"

Monk made a disgusted noise. "Well, we were back in that farmhouse, you know, where you left us to question them scamps. At first, they just called us Old English names. By the way, you'd be surprised at the names they can call you in that Old English language. Anyhow, before we got far with our rat-killing, some of their partners barged in on us unexpectedlike, and first thing you know, our names was mud. We wound up here."

"My question," Doc reminded Monk, "was this: What have you learned about this mystery?"

"Well," Monk said, "they recaptured some girl named Portia. It seems Portia had got away from another part of their gang, and they wanted her back. Portia was trying to get to you, and had sent some one to you, another girl named China——"

"Yes," Doc interrupted, "but what have you learned?"

"We're on a submarine."

"But what is this all about? What have you learned?"

"If you've got to be so darned persistent—nothing," Monk grumbled. "We ain't learned a thing."

"And with that," said Ham, who had taken no part in the conversation up to this point, "Monk hit the nail on the head. We're mystified."

"We're flopdoozled," Monk explained.

When Monk coined a word to explain a predicament, it was apt to be a bad fix he was describing. Doc Savage inquired, and learned there was no one else locked up with them. Their prison cell was a compartment in the submarine.

"About the young woman named Portia," Doc said. "Do you know where she is?"

"Oh, boy!" Monk said. "Ziggety! Hot dog!"

"From which we can gather," Doc Savage said dryly, "that you have seen the young lady. Where is she?"

"They put her on board this submarine," Monk advised. "Further than that, I don't know."

Doc Savage moved to the steel door of the steel compartment which was located slightly abaft of midships in the sub.

"It is time we were doing something about this," the bronze man said, "providing anything can be done about it."

Monk and Ham went silent. It was utterly dark in the metal cubby, their captors having neglected to supply the newly installed electric light socket with a bulb. The place smelled very new; also, there was a trace of ozone odor that electric welding machines leave in the vicinity of their operations.

It was dark, but it was by no means quiet. Hammers, riveters, grinders, and electric drills made an uproar that illustrated exactly what they meant when they said a place was as noisy as a boiler factory.

"If Doc gets us out of here," homely Monk muttered, "I'll buy the cigars."

THE scientific training which Doc Savage had received had been thorough and, of course, included some work aimed at developing his sense of touch, which was particularly important when it was necessary to do something in the dark.

As one exercise, Doc Savage had started out reading the conventional Braille raised-dots-on-paper printing of the blind, and had systematically decreased the size of the Braille letters until he could touch-read astonishingly small type.

It did not take him long to feel out the construction of the door. There was nothing to be encouraged about. The door would have been rather formidable equipment for a vault.

Doc took all the buttons off his coat, and crushed these separately, then mixed the powder. Then he tore his necktie in two pieces and used the ends to fashion receptacles for the powder on top of the door hinges. He poured the powder in the receptacles.

The bronze man then tore the lining out of the watch pocket of his trousers, wadded it, and rasped it along the wall as if he were striking a match. The cloth burst into flame. He applied this flame to the powder.

There was a loud, hissing noise and an incredibly white light; the hinges began to melt, and molten metal spilled down on the floor. The powder Doc had mixed was a form of thermite which was much hotter than the usual type formed by combining powdered aluminum and a metallic oxide.

While the special thermite was melting the hinges, Doc Savage grasped the door and shook it. It soon came loose, hinges melted away.

"Blazes!" Monk breathed. "We've got a start!"

Doc Savage lifted the door to one side and put his head out into the corridor. The coast was clear.

"Next," Doc said, "we find the two young women, Portia and China."

"But we'll have enough trouble," Monk reminded, "getting ourselves out of here."

"If we left them, and escaped, we might feel embarrassed," Doc Savage suggested.

"When I escape, I think I'll be too pleased to be embarrassed," Monk muttered. "However, where are these women?"

Doc said, "They may be in another one of these compartments."

THE bronze man and his aids ventured out into the corridor, still seeing no one but themselves, and began opening all the doors they came to. The steel doors did not have locks, but only the regulation arrangement of steel dogs with which they could be wedged water-tight. They could all be opened from the outside.

To fix the doors so they could not be opened from the inside, as in the case of the cubby from which Doc and his two men had just escaped, part of the closing mechanism was simply removed from the inside of the door.

Behind the seventh door they opened, they found Duchess Portia Montanye-Norwich.

Portia was exactly what the mind would naturally picture for a former showgirl who had married a wealthy duke, whose husband had died, and who had then become a rich thrill-seeker. She exactly filled the bill.

She was a tall, striking, dark-haired beauty of the Ziegfeld type. The light of adventure was in her wide, dark eyes; her mouth was shaped exactly right to taste thrills, and also to deliver them; and she carried herself as if ready for excitement.

Portia was hollow-eyed for want of sleep, and some rough handling had bedraggled her clothing; but she still gave the impression that, no matter what trouble she was in, she had done her part toward getting herself out of it.

Being rich, as well as a duchess, she was apparently accustomed to issuing orders. She lost no time giving one.

"Get me out of here!" she commanded imperiously.

China appeared beside Duchess Portia. China still wore her bathing suit. She gaped at Doc Savage.

"I'll bet," China said, "that they didn't turn you loose."

Doc Savage gave orders in a voice which did not sound particularly excited.

"We will go out through the conning tower," he said. "Run

for my car. Don't try to get out of the doors. Head for the car."

This proved to be a remarkably feasible plan until they stepped out of the conning tower. Two jumps took them to the movable stairs, and they clattered down those. Doc Savage took the lead, because opening a path was most important.

Prince Albert saw them. He let out a howl. Welders dropped torches, and every one else dropped whatever they were carrying. A charge for the fugitive began.

Surprisingly, Prince Albert howled orders to stop the escape without shooting if it could be done.

The charge closed in. Doc Savage straight-armed one man, then picked up the next one bodily and hurled him at a third. This got them to the car. Portia, China and Ham got into the machine. Then Doc Savage. Monk was last.

Monk had stopped to let the rush catch up with him, so he could hit somebody. Monk loved a fight. He knocked two men down, then turned and scrambled into the car; but before he got entirely in, a man had him by a heel.

Monk reached back with one of his remarkably long arms and stuck a finger in the man's eye, loosening the fellow's grip. Then Monk got in.

They slammed the car doors and locked themselves in the machine.

CHINA gasped for breath, then said, "I hope this car is what you fellows seem to think it is."

Outside, a rifle crashed, and the bullet hit a window, but only made a small pit and some spider web cracks. Prince Albert had evidently changed his mind about not firing off guns.

"You see," Monk told China.

A gas grenade rolled under the car and exploded with a rotten-egg smell. Several others followed. The men then ran around seizing up gas masks and gas suits where they had been laid aside.

Doc's car was gas proof, so there were no ill effects inside.

The bronze man got the motor started, meshed gears, and the car jumped forward. Three foes, fleeing its path, fell off the drydock runway into the water, which was below. Doc backed and turned around.

A hand grenade, high-explosive, let go on top of the car.

The car top dented like a tin can that had been kicked, and the concussion did agonizing things to the ears of those inside the automobile. But there were no serious effects.

Doc said, "Bump coming up!"

The car hit the door. It was doing about twenty, enough to shock them. The machine, being armor-plated, weighed a few tons, and would have demolished an ordinary door.

This one was not ordinary. The car bounced back from the door, and the portal looked almost as intact as before.

Doc hit it again. He was not gentle. The crash was terrific, and the breath was knocked out of all. The door still held.

Men were around the car now, shooting at the windows, the windshield, and the tires. Four men got on the front fenders and tried to get the hood open. The hood, however, was armor-plate that locked with a key.

Doc Savage jerked a lever on the dashboard, and chemical cylinders under the car poured out a cloud of black smoke mixed with anæsthetic gas. The gas would not have effect, because all the attackers now wore masks, but the smoke would hamper them.

The car hit the door a third time. And again, it was unsuccessful.

"That door," Doc Savage remarked, "cannot hold up all night."

"Neither," Ham croaked, "can we."

Doc backed up to give the door the hardest smash yet, and there was a rattling and clanking in the vicinity of the rear axle. The back of the car lifted off the concrete boathouse floor. The wheels merely spun.

A moment later, the car was hanging in the air by the rear axle. Doc knew, then, that some one had managed to attach the hook of a lifting crane to the axle, but it was too late for the knowledge to help much.

They dangled there, like a turkey hung up for picking, while their attackers waited until the chemical smoke was all gone, then got stepladders and electric drills and bored holes through the top of the car.

Through the holes in the top, the men poured gasoline. They used funnels. Monk tried to block the entry of the gasoline, but gave that up when they rammed an ice pick through the hole and damaged his hand.

When Prince Albert, yelling in a tone that left no doubt

about his meaning business, said blowtorches would be used to fire the inside of the car, Doc Savage and the others came out.

The bronze man was at once knocked unconscious.

Chapter X

RAIDERS

Doc Savage recovered consciousness, and decided he felt like a man who had taken a bath, and overdone the job. He felt as though he had been soaked too long and scrubbed hard.

After he sat up and examined himself, he decided the first impression had been right: He certainly appeared to have received a thorough laundering.

The bronze man wore nothing but a pair of underwear shorts which he had never seen before. His usually healthy-looking bronze skin was rough, raw—and scrubbed.

Glancing around, he perceived that Monk and Ham sat regarding him. Both wore long white gowns which were nothing more or less than old-fashioned nighties.

"I guess," Ham offered, "that they did not dope us as heavily as they did you. We've been awake about two days."

"How long?"

"Two days," Ham said.

"How many days since they got us out of the car?" Doc demanded.

Ham shook his head. "I don't know. Monk doesn't, either. They knocked you out, then took all your clothes off. They took our clothes, too. Then they gave us a scrubbing with soap and water and brushes——"

"I still think they used wire brushes to scrub with," Monk interrupted complainingly.

"Then," Ham continued, "they forced us to drink something that laid us all out."

"Mickey Finns," Monk explained.

Ham sighed. "I don't know how many times they scrubbed us when we were senseless. They were sure making certain we didn't have any more chemicals hidden on our persons."

54

Doc Savage nodded, and felt gingerly of his jaw. There was a general ache all through his teeth.

Monk said, "They took a chisel and a hammer and sounded out your teeth to make sure one of 'em wasn't a shell containing chemicals. If you've got a toothache, you know now what caused it."

Doc Savage got up rather painfully, took the blanket off the bunk, and hung it on a coat rack which was screwed fast to one steel bulkhead. He watched the blanket. When it swung from side to side, he knew the motion he had been feeling was not the result of his being dizzy.

"We are in the submarine," he announced.

Monk and Ham nodded.

"And we're at sea," Doc added.

"We're at sea, all right," Monk agreed. "And for how long, we don't know."

Doc asked, "Have they told you anything?"

Ham answered that. "They've told us plenty, none of it printable."

"I told you," Monk said, "that they can sure cuss in that old-time English they speak."

Ham put in, "That's a very funny thing, too. I thought at first they were acting, when they talked that way. Putting on. But I've concluded that is actually their normal speech."

"Figure that one out, if you can," Monk said.

Doc Savage navigated around the steel-walled submarine compartment several times, and got his sea legs, after which he discovered that he had been provided with a white flannel nightie such as Monk and Ham wore. He put this on.

Doc Savage went over and whacked the door with a fist, rattled the fastenings. After he had been engaged in doing this for a few minutes, the door suddenly snapped open a crack.

Doc gave it a great yank, but it would open no more than a crack because it had been equipped with a chain on the outside. A man outside chucked a small tear gas bomb through the crack, then yanked the door shut and fastened it again.

Doc, Monk and Ham sat down and babied their streaming eyes.

"The same thing happened to us," Monk explained.

Modern tear gas is a marvelous quieting influence, having been concocted on the order of police and industrial guards as a last resort in pacifying mobs.

It was a full fifteen minutes before Doc Savage and his two men felt like going on with any kind of discussion.

"If we could just make head or tail of this," Ham complained, "it would be different."

"Listen, shyster," Monk said, "I don't see where the difference would be. We'd still be in here, wouldn't we?"

"We'd have peace of mind," Ham retorted. "You're not equipped to understand that."

"I get it," Monk said. "You mean I ain't got a mind. Listen, you ambulance-chaser——"

"One angle is clear," Doc interrupted.

Doc had perceived that Monk and Ham were starting one of their quarrels which, like taxes, would go on and on. He wished to discourage this. When one had been associated more or less continuously with the Monk-and-Ham quarrel for a period of years, it could get monotonous.

"What angle is that?" Ham demanded.

"That shipyard," Doc Savage said, "is one of several that builds submarines for the United States navy. There were four navy subs under construction outside that boathouse."

"We saw them," Ham admitted.

"Did you notice," Doc asked, "how this submarine—providing this is the one that was in the boathouse——"

"It is," Ham said. "We heard them say so."

Doc continued, "Did you notice how it was being put together? All the parts seemed ready-made. It looked as if they had all the parts ready, and were throwing the U-boat together in a hurry."

"Say!" Ham exclaimed. "What do you reckon that means?"

"My guess," Doc stated, "would be that, as they built a navy submarine, they made a duplicate set of parts. Instead of stamping one hull plate, they would stamp two."

"In other words," Ham gasped, "they made one submarine for the U. S. navy, and another one exactly like it for somebody else?"

"That seems to be it," Doc said, "in view of the fact that the submarine which blew up off Boston harbor was an exact duplicate of another submarine, the U. S. S. *Swordfish!*"

Doc Savage had been sitting on the bunk, and now he got

up and took off his long nightie. He borrowed the nighties which Monk and Ham wore. He balled them together, added the blanket, and made a tight wad.

Next, he beat on the door, yelled, rattled the door fastenings. He kept it up for about five minutes. As before, the door flew open, and the guard pegged a gas bomb inside.

But this time, Doc Savage jammed his bundle into the door so that it could not be yanked shut again. He picked up the hot, steaming gas grenade, and threw it back into the corridor. Then he pulled the wad of nighties and blanket out of the crack and got the door shut.

There was a great deal of profanity as the tear gas spread through the submarine.

"A dose of their own medicine," Doc Savage said dryly.

PEACE descended on the submarine. Or as much peace as could descend on a sub at sea. The underseas craft apparently ran into a gale, because its antics became distressing.

The sub would begin to rise slowly and tremulously, writhing and groaning a little as if impaled on a spear, and on the crest of the wave it would hang suspended, then go plunging for the bottom. On these down trips, it had the habit of practically rolling over, one way or another.

The galley was evidently close by. Cooking odors from this made the air thick enough, Monk vowed to cut a slice and broil it.

Monk made a number of other remarks concerning the ancestry of submarines. He was seasick.

Having been relieved of every personal possession, including watches, the only way the prisoners could judge time was by the frequence with which they were fed. By this clock, five days had passed when the submarine refueled from a mother ship.

The sea was calm on the occasion, and the submarine apparently lay alongside a steamer, because there was an occasional shock and a groaning of fenders as the underseas boat rolled against the ship.

The crew clattered around on deck, attaching hose feed lines, after which fuel gurgled into the sub tanks for a long period.

Later, the submarine got under way again.

"What," Ham said, astonished, "do you make of that?"

"It don't encourage me any," groaned the seasick Monk. "It looks like we're in for a long voyage."

"What I meant," Ham remarked, "is this: They must have a considerable organization. A fuel ship meeting them at sea! Think of it!"

"You think!" Monk gulped. "I've got my stomach to think about."

Later, when the door opened a crack in the usual fashion, and their food was shoved inside, there was a scuffle in the corridor. A man swore.

Doc Savage, whipping forward, grasped the edge of the door, braced himself, and held the door open. He managed to keep it open against the efforts of those outside until two animals popped through the aperture. The new arrivals were Monk's pig, Habeas Corpus, and Ham's mascot runt ape, Chemistry.

Through the door crack, Prince Albert ordered angrily that the two animals be put out outside again. Monk and Ham replied with detailed instructions about where he could go, and some predictions about the temperature after he got there.

Prince Albert voiced a few of his own opinions. Monk pegged a dish of oatmeal through the door crack at him. After which Prince Albert closed the portal, and the incident as well.

An instant after the door closed, Doc Savage was on his knees beside Habeas. He inspected the pig. Then he examined the runt ape, Chemistry.

After that, the bronze man unconsciously brought into existence the strange, low, exotic trilling sound which he habitually made in moments of intense mental activity. The trilling was imbued with a definitely pleased quality.

"This," the bronze man said, "is a piece of luck."

Chapter XI

DANDRUFF

THE cannon went off at ten minutes until noon. Doc and his aids were sure about the time; what happened left no doubt. Their idea of the passing of time had gotten off enough that they thought it was still night, so they were asleep.

The big gun made a thump and a bang, and they rolled out of the bunks in a hurry. The heavy gun rolled the sub again with its recoil. This time, they knew it was a cannon.

Prince Albert yelled in the corridor.

He said, "Give 'em until noon to make up their minds. That'll be ten minutes!"

So they knew the time was ten minutes until noon.

There was a period of silence, followed by banging noises on the hull. This sounded as if some one was going around silently giving the hull plates a terrific blow here and there with a hammer.

"You know what I think?" Ham gasped.

"Bullets," Doc Savage said.

"Exactly. They shot at some one with the cannon. And that some one is shooting back with rifles."

Doc Savage's metallic features were expressionless, but his feelings were evidently the same as those being shown by Monk and Ham: blank astonishment.

They heard the submarine's deck gun go off three times in rapid succession. Following this, there was another silence. The engines of the submarine stopped completely.

For approximately an hour, the submarine lay rolling in the swells. Amid clattering uproar, a boat was apparently taken out of a deck compartment and placed in the water. It went away, and came back in twenty minutes. It made two more round trips to wherever it was going.

The small boat was then swung into its deck compartment,

stowed, and the submarine engines started. The sub maneuvered for a while.

There was a windy cough of a noise.

"Torpedo!" Ham barked. "They've fired a torpedo!"

"*Sh-h-h!*" Monk breathed.

Monk's shushing was not necessary. He wanted to listen for the torpedo to strike. All held their breaths.

The torpedo struck. No doubt of that. The explosion was deep and booming, and almost as much of a shock as a blast.

Engines of the submarine speeded up then, and the craft began to travel at high speed, bumping into the larger swells with noticeable shocks.

Doc Savage and the other two sat silent, mentally contemplating what had happened.

"They torpedoed a ship," Monk muttered.

"But first," said Ham, "they halted it with shell-fire."

"Yeah. They went aboard, too."

"Made three trips," Ham admitted. "Then they socked a torpedo into her."

"It's kind of crazy," Monk mumbled.

"It's fantastic!" Ham exploded.

"It wouldn't be so hard to savvy," Monk explained, "if there was a war going on."

"But there's no war," Ham finished.

Doc Savage had been taking slow turns about the tiny steel cubicle, putting out a hand to brace himself against the rolling motion. Now he stopped.

"The war," he said, "is the important part, I believe, that we have overlooked."

Monk asked, "What do you mean? There ain't no war."

"But there is fighting going on," Doc reminded.

"Oh, sure. Like that Spanish trouble. And the mess in China. But they haven't declared war——" Monk suddenly stopped speaking, swallowed with difficulty, and gulped, "Blazes!"

The homely chemist ran fingers through his hair and down hard on the back of his neck. His pleasantly terrifying face worked into various shapes.

"Doc!" he exploded. "I've got it! Fighting in Europe! Undeclared wars. Ships firing on each other. Rumors of pirate submarines. *Pirate submarines!* Isn't that what you mean?"

"Pirate submarines," Doc Savage said, "is worth a thought."

THE newspapers had carried, from time to time, stories about mysterious attacks on ships which were made by submarines of unidentified nationality. First attacks had occurred in the neighborhood of the Mediterranean. They had not been confined to the Mediterranean entirely, however.

Doc Savage and his two men were silent, considering the various aspects of the startling possibility they had just unearthed.

"Pirates!" Ham exclaimed. "The thing is fantastic! This is the Twentieth Century!"

"It's against my policy to agree with you," Monk told Ham. "But it does look like a fuzzy idea. Pirates went out of style with Captain Kidd."

Doc Savage pointed out some facts. "The nations of Europe," he reminded, "have been engaged in a rearmament and intrigue for a number of years. They are like neighbors who think they're going to have to fight each other, and who have been hiding shotguns and revolvers in their houses, yet trying to keep the neighbors from knowing about the guns or where they are hidden. But nobody wants to start fighting.

"Consequently, when a gun goes off by accident, everybody denies it would have happened in his house. The European nations are like that. It accounts for the air of mystery that surrounded those mysterious submarine attacks."

Monk took several large swallows of air. "Doc, you think some nation is sponsoring these pirates?"

"Not necessarily," the bronze man said. "Suppose some remarkable Twentieth Century pirate got enough men together, got submarines, and started raiding. The international situation is ideal. Suppose the pirate sank a German ship? The Germans would naturally suspect the Russians did it, because Germany is not too friendly with Russia."

The aids discussed this, and began to see how logical it was. It became more likely when Doc pointed out that the pirates of the Spanish Main used exactly the same tactics. Spain was at war with England at the time, and when the Spaniards lost a ship, they were inclined to blame the English.

"But," said Monk, "how do you account for these pirates talking Old-English lingo?"

"And where does this Duchess Portia come in?" Ham added.

"We might sleep on that part of the mystery," Doc suggested.

Doc and his aids got up the next morning, compared results of deliberations, and decided no conclusions had been reached. Things remained at this stalemate for five more days.

ON the evening of the fifth day, the submarine abruptly stopped its characteristic mad rolling, and the engines went dead. A loud rasping of chain from the bows indicated the anchor was being dropped.

"We've made port," Ham decided.

"What port?" Monk inquired unreasonably.

The door of their prison opened as much as the chain would permit.

"I have words for you gentlemen," Prince Albert said from a safe distance up the corridor.

"I've got something for you, too," Monk assured him. "Some day, I hope to give it to you."

"With interest, I suppose."

"With enthusiasm!"

Prince Albert chuckled sourly. "You guys have been a pain. If it was up to me, I'd have fixed you up with caskets long ago. But the big boss says different. He's got plans for you."

"Got what?" Monk demanded.

"Plans," Prince Albert said. "Now don't start askin' me what. Explainin' always gives me a headache."

"Have you got somethin' to say?" Monk asked.

"Sure," admitted Prince Albert. "I'm just tellin' you to sit on any ideas you got about makin' trouble, and you'll be all right. Maybe not all right, but you'll be alive. Which is more'n you'll be if you start messin' around again."

"Are we going to be left in here?" asked Doc Savage, who had taken no part in the conversation up to now.

"You bet," Prince Albert said, and gave orders for the door to be locked again.

Doc Savage relaxed on the bunk. He indicated that it would not be a bad idea for Monk and Ham to do the same thing.

"It is probably about dusk now," the bronze man said in a low voice. "We will wait about four hours, and we might as well get some sleep."

Monk and Ham looked much interested.

"By any chance," Monk muttered, "you wouldn't be taking that guy's advice not to mess around?"

"We wouldn't be," Doc said.

Doc Savage then went to sleep, to the secret disgust of Monk and Ham, who lay wide awake and wondered what the bronze man was figuring on doing. Having had more than two weeks to consider the possibilities of their escaping, they considered them very slender.

IN almost exactly four hours, Doc awakened. He caught the pet Habeas with his right hand, and the runt ape Chemistry with his left hand, and put both animals on the bunk.

Habeas and Chemistry did not enjoy being in close proximity. They got along together about as well as Monk and Ham, their respective owners.

Doc began to rub the backs of the two animals together. Habeas squealed. Chemistry squalled. Doc kept on rubbing.

"I don't think," Monk decided, watching the pets, "that is gonna make 'em any better friends. When you turn 'em loose, that hog is gonna to eat up that other thing."

Ham snorted. "Any time your bacon rind eats Chemistry, he'll know he's been to the banquet."

Doc Savage now gave Habeas Corpus to Monk. The homely chemist held his outraged pet by one enormous ear. Doc removed his shirt, spread it on the bunk, held Chemistry over it, and gave the remarkable ape's fur what is known in juvenile parlance as a "Dutch rub." A shower of grayish powder fell on the shirt.

"Dandruff?" Ham asked.

"Not exactly," Doc corrected. "A precipitate caused by the union of a chemical painted on Chemistry's fur, and on Habeas's bristles."

Monk made a startled noise. "When'd you paint 'em, Doc?"

"The stuff has been kept on the pets for several months," Doc explained. "This is the first time we have needed to try it out."

"What's the object of the powder?" demanded Monk.

Doc said, "Watch."

He shook the powder he had collected from the shirt to the palm of his right hand. Then he pounded on the door with his left hand.

"Silence, thou!" ordered a quarrelsome-voiced guard out-side.

"We have something important for you," Doc called. "It should be given to your leader, as well."

After some hesitating, the guard opened the door the usual crack. Doc came close to the aperture. The guard was Henry.

Henry looked, if possible, longer and sourer than usual. He could see that the bronze man's hands held no weapon.

Doc started to speak, acted as if he had to cough to clear his throat, pretended to be polite, and brought his right hand up and coughed into it. He coughed out enough air to blow the powder into Henry's vinegary face.

Henry could not help inhaling the powder.

"I'm awfully sorry," Doc apologized quickly.

Henry apparently decided he had to sneeze, and he took in a tremendous breath with that intention. His sneeze, when it came off, was rather a dud. Henry seemed dazed.

Doc reached through the door crack, got Henry, pulled him close, and hung a right hook on the fellow's jaw. Henry went slack.

"Yeow!" Monk said in a low, vehement voice. "If Henry's only got the keys to the padlock on that chain!"

Henry had the keys, and the aids unfastened the chain, got the door opened, and stepped into the steel-walled cor-ridor. They locked Henry in the prison they were vacating.

Chapter XII

RAIDER ISLAND

A GUARD sat on the threshold of the conning tower hatch, smoking a cigarette. The hatch was more after the fashion of a door in the side of the conning tower superstructure. The guard seemed to be enjoying his smoke. He took the cigarette from his lips, held it out and eyed it deliciously.

When Monk socked the guard, the cigarette flew out of the fellow's fingers, hit the deck, made a shower of sparks, and sailed on into the dark water.

"You hit him too hard!" Ham accused Monk.

"I was illustratin'," Monk chuckled.

"Illustrating?"

"I hit 'im," Monk said cheerfully, "the way I'm gonna sock you some day."

Monk and Ham dragged their senseless prize down the conning tower steps into the engine room, where Doc Savage was making an examination.

"There was only the two of 'em aboard," Monk explained. "The others must've gone ashore. After that trip we had, I don't blame 'em."

Doc Savage completed his examination. He made his low, trilling sound, but it was subdued, and lasted only an instant. It had a disgusted tone.

"We can't make off with the sub," the bronze man explained.

Monk frowned. "Why not?"

"They've removed essential parts of the engines."

Monk groaned. "They don't overlook bets, do they?"

Doc Savage got pliers and a small wrench from the tool racks and took from the big Diesel engines some further parts which would insure them remaining inoperative. These being too heavy to swim ashore with, he put them in a blanket, tied a wire around the blanket and left about thirty feet of the wire dangling.

Stripping off his nightshirt, Doc went on deck, slid over the side, and tied the end of the wire to an elevator fin, leaving the engine parts to dangle below the surface, where they might not be found.

Monk and Ham in the meantime had searched the sub for weapons. The best they could find were butcher knives out of the gallery. They came out on deck, and Monk put one foot in the water.

"*Br-r!*" he gasped.

"Not as warm as it might be," Doc Savage admitted. "Just a minute. Let's see if we can find where we are."

The usual navigating instruments—sextant and chronometer—were in the captain's cabin. Doc carried these on deck, and took a star shot.

While the bronze man was below making his calculations, Monk and Ham looked the situation over from the deck, using night glasses.

They accomplished little. It was very dark, and clouds obscured most of the stars. They got the impression that the submarine lay in a small bay which was surrounded on all sides by high stone cliffs.

Doc called to them in a low voice.

"We're on a small island in a very remote part of the Atlantic," he explained.

BOTH guards now regained consciousness, and promptly began yelling at the top of their voices. Monk put a stop to that with a great deal of glee.

"Doc, do you want to know what this is all about?" Monk demanded.

"Somewhat," the bronze man admitted.

"O. K.," Monk said. "I'll ask our two guests."

"They'll be likely to tell you, you missing link!" interjected Ham.

"In that case," Monk advised, "I'll pull off fingers and things."

The homely chemist was not as bloodthirsty as he sounded. He was implying that he was a holy terror for the effect.

Beginning to question the prisoners, he endeavored to keep up the illusion.

As a last resort, he even twisted a couple of fingers out of joint of each guard. This was harmless, but very painful. It did not get results.

The two guards would say absolutely nothing.

Doc Savage bound the fellows, and locked them in the compartment from which he and his men has escaped. As Monk remarked, "We know just how hard it is to get outta there!"

Doc said, "It is important to see what we can find on shore."

Monk thought of the cold bay water. *"Br-r-r!"* he said.

Doc Savage examined the layout of the sub's controls.

"The tanks," Doc decided, "can be filled, then blown. The vessel can be submerged, then brought back to the surface. Let's see how deep the bay is."

They put a sounding lead over the rail and got a depth of slightly over fifteen fathoms with a sand bottom.

"Less than a hundred feet," Doc remarked. "We can submerge and lie on the bottom."

Monk looked puzzled. "But what good will that do us? Just sitting under the water won't help the situation."

Doc had searched the forward compartments of the submarine, and Monk and Ham had not visited that portion of the craft as yet.

"The boat is equipped with an escape compartment," Doc explained. "A diver can leave the craft, and also return, through the compartment."

"Oh!" Monk said.

Doc and his aids filled the ballast tanks of the submarine and sank her where she lay at anchor. The craft was modern, and so equipped that she could be submerged silently in time of war. They got down without a great deal of noise. Finally, there was a bump that indicated they were on the bottom.

The escape compartment was a small water-tight chamber with two hatches. One hatch opened into the submarine. The other opened out of the submarine hull to the sea. There were two sets of valves in the compartment. One set let in the sea. The other valve set blew it out with compressed air.

Doc Savage climbed into the compartment. He took no weapons.

WATER came into the escape compartment, when Doc forced open the outer door with the mechanical arrangement for that purpose, with almost the force of buckshot. Air, of course, had to go somewhere, and doubtless it reached the surface in the form of huge bubbles. Whether these would attract attention from shore was a question.

Pressure at the depth was more startling than dangerous. The bronze man had been down to greater depths on other occasions, and he took the agony in his ears, the sensation of a horse standing on his chest, for granted. He stroked for the top, and as the pressure slackened, he was aware of the cold.

There was a little oil slick on the bay surface where the U-boat had submerged, but tide would carry that away. There was, the bronze man realized, a very definite tide motion.

He took bearings on the rugged shore, aligning it with a couple stars in the sky beyond. He gave himself plenty of time for that. It was important to find the submarine again.

While he was taking observations, Doc saw a brief light on shore. It was a flashlight beam, white as a fleeting ghost, and brief. He swam toward the light, keeping his strokes beneath the surface.

The beach was solid rock, cold, hard and dark. Waves breaking in stony cracks and pitholes sounded like dogs snarling. Crawling out on the dark lava rock, Doc removed his only garments, underwear and shorts, wrung them out, wiped himself nearly dry with them, wrung them out again, and put them back on.

By then, the bronze man had heard sounds. They came from the shore to his right, and were obviously noises made by men getting in a small boat. A moment later, a speed boat motor started, and the craft ran out on the bay, a scudding black spot chased by a frothing white tail of wake.

A searchlight beam jumped from the boat to the spot where the submarine should have been. Of course, there was no submarine.

"They've stolen the hooker!" Prince Albert's voice bellowed.

THE searchlight lunged like a hungry-hunting thing over the bay. Waves squirmed in the white light, and the cliffs stood like black walls when it touched them, so that the bay seemed something macabre, like a setting for a weird film created on a movie set.

The launch, having scanned the harbor, went charging out through a gap in the stone cliffs, a gap so narrow as to be nearly unnoticeable, which evidently led out to sea.

Judging from the quickness with which the launch came charging back in again, the sea outside was too rough for the small boat. In fact, Doc had noticed a steady undertone of rumbling of surf breaking on the shores of the island.

The bronze man was close to a stone wharf when the launch surged in and men sprang ashore with lines. Several flashlights were turned on in the craft, and illuminated Prince Albert's route as he got ashore.

The squat, homely Prince Albert wore skin-tight breeches of mouse-colored cloth, high stockings, shoes with big buckles, and his loose gray shirt had a ruffled collar and pleated sleeves. He carried a long rapier in a scabbard at his waist.

The sight of him would undoubtedly have given Monk a spasm.

"Couriers, ho!" Prince Albert shouted.

The command brought a clatter of hoofs, and a squad of horsemen galloped into the flashlight glow. The mounted men wore armor, had tall plumes in their helmets, and carried long lances, swords, and enormous horse pistols.

They made a spectacle that would have fitted better into a motion picture of medieval times.

"Tell the master," Prince Albert shouted, "that they have freed themselves, taken the submarine and fled with it!"

"Aye, sire!"

"Tell him we'd better get the planes ready to go out and search at dawn."

"Aye, sire!" And there was a clamor of hoofbeats as the horse party departed.

Doc Savage at once advanced on Prince Albert and his group, with the intention of picking them off one at a time in the darkness.

But Prince Albert must have been nervous. He ordered his men to point their flashlight beams outward, and they did this, so that they were surrounded with bright light. There was no way Doc Savage could get close to them without being seen.

The horsemen came galloping back. They carried smoking torches which were probably made out of pitch knots.

"Ho!" shouted the spokesman.

"Ho, yourself!" Prince Albert grumbled. "What'd the boss say?"

"The boss says, sire, that thou hast let grass grow on thy wits," advised the courier.

"Eh?"

"The submarine would'st not run."

"The hell it would'st not! Do you see it out there? It's gone, ain't it?"

"Nay, sire," advised the courier. "Dost it not occur that the craft was merely submerged while still at anchor?"

This was such an obvious deduction that Prince Albert began swearing at his own stupidity. He had, as he demonstrated on other occasions, a large, well-colored vocabulary.

"Get bloodhounds!" he howled. "Get our dogs. Savage and his men may try to make the shore. And get depth bombs! We'll bring 'em up, or keep 'em down there for good!"

The horsemen dashed off again, and shortly after they disappeared, there came the excited baying of dogs. When the riders came back, they were surrounded by noisy, excited hounds.

Hardly had the dogs arrived when sudden silence seized the pack. They made snuffling noises. In the flashlight's glow, Doc Savage could see the animals facing slowly toward where he was hidden. They were enormous dogs. Several looked as big as Shetland ponies. One dog bayed like a good-sized foghorn.

It was time to be doing something.

As nearly without noise as he could manage, the bronze man eased backward. He angled toward the bay. If he could get into the water and swim and come out somewhere else, the pack might not be able to trail him.

Silence was difficult. Underfoot there was stone, and all around boulders, great house-sized stones, and a little, a very little vegetation, mostly stunted shrubs.

It was poor country for flight, also very dark. The bronze man moved with long steps, hands out in front, feeling.

The hounds were clamoring now, trailing him. The echo of their bawling and yapping pulsed back from the cliffs of the bay, sounding strangely human; it was like the free-for-all hog-calling contests at mid-West country fairs, where all the candidates call hogs at once.

Suddenly Doc knew he wouldn't make it. The hounds knew

their work; three or four wise heads had circled to cut him off.

The bronze man was gouged by hard limbs of a stunted tree. He climbed into that. The shrub was an evergreen, hardly large enough for a respectable Christmas tree, and he wrapped himself around topmost boughs.

A moment later, the big dogs were jumping into the tree and floundering around among its branches. Their roars were like those of lions.

Flashlight beams tilted around like crazy lances as the horsemen arrived on the scene. Men in armor waded among the animals with staves and long whips that popped like small revolvers; the armor had seemed silly up to this point, but around these dogs it was a practical necessity.

The men probably wore it on account of the bloodhounds. It seemed to make no difference to the big dogs whom they attacked. They went after their masters as enthusiastically as after Doc Savage.

Finally the men got leashes on the animals.

Prince Albert spurred close to the scrub tree and poked Doc Savage with the end of the lance.

"This reminds me," Prince Albert said gleefully, "of possum hunts we used to have in Arkansas."

Doc Savage kept silent.

"Hang one of your legs down where we can reach it," Prince Albert ordered.

Doc Savage did that, after hesitating. They put a leg iron around his ankle and padlocked it. There was all of forty feet of chain attached to this leg iron. A man made the chain end fast to a saddle.

"Drag him!" Prince Albert yelled. "We'll take out his ambition!"

The man with the end of the chain spurred his horse, and the animal leaped. Doc Savage flung himself out of the tree. He was not enthusiastic about being dragged; the sharp rocks could rip a man.

Holding up his end of the chain with both hands, the bronze man scrambled twice around the base of the tree, then braced himself holding his end of the chain wrapped around the trunk.

The horseman came to the end of the chain, lost his spear, parted company with his horse, and landed in the rocks. He sounded, encased in his armor, as though some one had dropped a sack of tin cans.

The remaining men prodded the bronze man to his feet with lances.

"You're more danged trouble!" Prince Albert complained.

Doc's captors did not try to drag him again. They led him along a path which passed through a wilderness of boulders, skirted the base of a great rocky peak, then climbed obliquely up the face of the peak.

On the right, the peak went up as sheer as the side of a skyscraper. To the left was black space. After several hundred yards, they came to a break in the path—a gap where there was no trail at all for a distance greater than any man or animal could hope to leap.

"Let the draw down!" Prince Albert shouted.

"Aye, sire," came from the other side.

Winches creaked, chains rattled, and a drawbridge of heavy timbers, almost two score feet in length, settled into the gap. After the party crossed the drawbridge, a path climbed even more steeply. Then there were steps, wide steps which the horses could mount.

"What he don't know won't hurt 'im!" Prince Albert said suddenly. "Blindfold him."

A coat was wrapped around the bronze man's head and lashed there so that he could see nothing more. Then he was thrown across a horse, and the animal climbed steps; later, the hoofbeats and voices vibrated in a hollow way which told Doc that they were in a passage, and finally, he was hauled off the horse.

There was a grating noise as if a stone trapdoor was being opened. The bronze man was lifted and tossed into space.

He fell far enough to strike very heavily, and after he had explored, he knew that he had landed on the bottom of a pit that was floored at least a foot deep with sand that was as fine as talcum powder.

Chapter XIII

SLAVES

APPROXIMATELY an hour passed, but when this hour was about half gone there were seven shocks, extremely faint; seven times when the earth seemed to jar. After the first two came, Doc Savage put an ear to the stone pit wall, listened to the others, and his metallic face went grim, for the shocks were undoubtedly distant explosions.

He thought of his two men in the sub, and what depth bombs would do to the craft. And at the end of the hour, the stone hatch opened.

"Things coming down!" Prince Albert called gleefully.

Monk and Ham were pitched through the ceiling hole. They landed heavily beside Doc Savage. The bronze man gave them a little time to get their breath back.

"Any serious damage?" the bronze man asked.

"Doc!" Monk exploded. "Did you see them dogs they got? They're ornery as lions!"

"How did they get you out of the submarine?"

"Depth bombs," Monk grumbled.

Ham said, "They started setting off the charges systematically. There was nothing we could do but come up. And besides, they took our pets with them. They're not taking any chances."

"Doc, did you get a look at this place?" Monk demanded. "Or did they blindfold you, too?"

The bronze man admitted that he had been blindfolded.

The stone hatch overhead was shut by now, and the color of the air around them was approximately that of drawing ink.

Monk waded around in the sand feeling things over with his hands. "Hey, Doc! We're in a cistern!" He scooped up the powder-fine sand. "What's this stuff? Believe I'll taste it. Phooey! Sand!"

"Fat chance we've got climbing out of here," Ham complained.

Unexpectedly the hatch reopened. Prince Albert tossed something down, and it struck Monk.

"Ouch!" Monk complained. He felt the object. "A funnel! Hey, up there, what's the idea?"

Prince Albert's chuckle was as nasty as the growl of one of the big dogs. "Feel around the wall about neck-high. You'll find a hole. Put the funnel in the hole."

"Then what?"

"Use your own judgment," Prince Albert said. He dropped the hatch.

An instant later, there was a hissing noise and a steady stream of fine sand came pouring down from an aperture somewhere in the ceiling.

Monk sneezed. He hit at the falling sand with his hands and grunted, puzzled. "I don't get this!!"

"Just strain your imagination a little, you freak!" Ham suggested.

Monk made explosive noises, then hunted frantically for the funnel and located the hole Prince Albert had mentioned. Thereafter, they took turns at the monotonous task of pouring sand into the funnel.

Unless they kept the sand level down, there was nothing to prevent the stuff from filling the pit and suffocating them.

"Talk about your pouring sand in rat holes!" Monk grumbled.

IT must have been several hours later—long enough so that it was surely daylight outside—when Prince Albert cut off the sand and opened the hatch.

"I see you've been kept out of mischief," he remarked. He tossed down a bundle which proved to hold loose white gowns. "Put those on."

They put the garments on.

Prince Albert sent a knotted rope down. "Climb it," he invited.

When Doc and his aids climbed out of the pit, they were surrounded by men with lances and short swords.

"Hello," Doc Savage said expressionlessly.

"Hello," China replied without much enthusiasm.

The showgirl stood with two men holding her wrists, one of

whom had a black eye, apparently of recent origin. China looked very downcast.

The homely Monk looked at the showgirl and tried to cheer her up.

"It could be worse, you know," Monk suggested.

"That," China said, "is just what you think!"

Doc Savage's flake gold eyes went sharply to the young woman. He got the impression that she had very recently received a shock.

"What is it?" the bronze man asked.

"Prepare yourself," China said, "for a shock!"

"Meaning?"

The girl parted her lips to speak and trembled; she pinched them tightly together, and tears came into her eyes. Suddenly, she kicked at the men who held her and tried to bite them; when she could do neither, she buried her face in her arms and burst into wild sobs.

"Women," Prince Albert remarked, "hate to be fooled."

Two men dragging China took the lead, and the others followed a double column in their wake, shoving along Doc Savage, Monk and Ham.

The group traversed an arched stone corridor, and this opened into a room of considerable size, with ceiling beams made of whole logs; they crossed this room, passed through a wide door and marched forward on a strip of velvet carpet so purple it was almost black, and across the floor to a huge room with a large dais. Monk peered at the object on the dais and licked his lips.

He muttered, "That's all we needed to top this off!"

He referred to the throne on the dais, and to the fact that the thing looked as if it might be made of gold. When the march stopped at the foot of the dais, Monk attempted to go on and get a close look at the throne. He was hauled back. Some one gave him a whack with the flat of a sword.

"I was just tryin' to find out," the homely chemist grumbled, "if that thing is solid gold."

"Restrain yourself, pest!" Prince Albert ordered. "The boss is gonna hold court in a minute."

"Is it gold?"

"No, of course not."

"All right," Monk growled. "Court—whatcha mean by 'court'?"

"Shut up!" Prince Albert requested.

Then all Doc's group stared in astonishment at the person who was coming through the door.

The Duchess Portia Montanye-Norwich appeared and walked toward the throne with regal hauteur, not looking right or left.

China whispered, "Now you know what got my goat!"

NEITHER Doc Savage nor his men looked at each other.

Monk said, "She's——" and could not finish.

China said, "That's right. She's it."

"But——"

"Believe it or not," China said, "she's it. And I didn't know it, either."

"She deceived you?"

"*Deceived* is a mild word for it!" China flared. "The stuck-up tramp!" China took hold of her lower lip with her teeth and gave it a bite. "She used to be swell people. That's what fooled me."

Monk began loudly, "But back there in New York——"

The flat of the sword smacked Monk again. He went silent.

"That squeak of yours irritates me!" Prince Albert growled.

Monk said, "I'll be danged——" and the flat of the sword smacked him again, so he changed his mind and remained silent.

The Duchess Portia seated herself, made a signal with her right hand, and Prince Albert turned back the edge of the velvet carpet to reveal a number of iron rings fixed in the floor at regular intervals. Doc Savage's two men and China were chained to these convenient anchorages.

The guards then retired, Prince Albert included.

Doc Savage tested the strength of the ring to which he was chained, found it disappointingly solid; and Monk and Ham, after giving their chains two or three yanks, threw the chains on the stone floor with a great clatter, resigning themselves. They fell to examining the Duchess Portia.

This morning the lady was strikingly attired in a loose, flowing white silk thing caught at the waist with a purple cord. She wore a cape of white, and her sandals were open enough to show that her toenails were tinted. She was something that would make an impression on almost any masculine eye.

"You don't look like a female Dracula," Monk remarked.

The comment apparently irked Portia.

"You will speak," she said sharply, "when you're spoken to!"

Ignoring the instructions, Doc Savage said, "Back in New York, you seemed to be in need of help."

"I did that act rather well, don't you think?" Portia asked coolly.

"You mean that you put on an *act* in New York?"

"Exactly."

Doc Savage looped his leg chain and hung it over an arm, while he thought over what she had said.

"What was the object of the acting?"

"To get you here," Portia said briefly.

"Get us?"

"Exactly." Portia gave the side of the throne an impatient tap with her fingers. "Off Boston harbor, our other submarine blew up unexpectedly. It was an accident. I was rescued.

"After I got ashore, I went ahead with the plan which I had come to America to execute: a plan to seize you and your men and bring you here. To do that, it was necessary to deceive you." She curled her lip scornfully. "You see, I knew about your profession of helping people."

"And why did you want us here?"

Duchess Portia showed them her teeth; she probably intended it for a smile.

"I presume you have some idea of what we're doing here?"

"Some," Doc admitted.

"Good!" Portia said. "Then you'll understand when I tell you that we're going to throw the blame for the whole thing on to you."

"But——"

Portia raised her voice and called, "Put them on the chain gang. Take the girl and bring her to my chamber to act as maid!"

Prince Albert came in with his men and unlocked the chains from the floor rings. China was led away before Doc and his men were freed.

"This'll be a new experience for you," Prince Albert said cheerfully.

Chapter XIV

HENRY'S DILEMMA

Doc and his little group could hear the groaning sound long before they reached it, and at first they thought it was something of mechanical origin, so regularly did it rise and fall; so much was it like the noise of a machine.

At first, though, they missed the true significance of the sound; not until they had traversed a long corridor and passed through a heavy door in the outer castle wall did the pulsing vehemence of the sound begin to impress them.

Then, after they had been shoved unexpectedly into blinding outdoor day, they blinked owlishly and looked around; for moments they stared in astonishment.

Above them, to a towering height, lifted stone walls that were rugged, forbidding, and jutted out at intervals in turrets, and were fanged along the top with archery embrasures.

Monk made the first remark.

"In my kid history books, there was a picture," the homely chemist muttered. "It was labeled 'Building the Pyramids by Man Power.'"

"Get movin'!" Prince Albert ordered. "You ain't here for the sights!"

They were shoved toward the groaning men.

It was not exactly a groaning. There were at least sixty of the men, all chained to a huge wooden sled which was being dragged up the path. Stone blocks were piled on the sled, and the groaning noise seemed to be an expedient to keep time so that the human draft horses could yank together.

"Seems to me," Monk complained, "they'd feel better if they grunted somethin' cheerful."

Prince Albert snorted, "Yank that thing all day, and see how easy it is to be cheerful!"

Doc Savage and his men were added to the chain gang by

78

the simple expedient of having the ends of their chains padlocked to the sled.

"Now you pull on the chains," Prince Albert explained.

MONK opened his large mouth, the expression on his homely face indicating that he had a great deal to say on the subject of pulling sleds—but he only popped his small eyes at a man chained to the sled immediately behind them.

"Henry!" Monk exclaimed.

"Our old friend, Henry!" Ham echoed.

The long, red-headed Henry gave them a pained look. He was, like themselves, attired in a shapeless gown.

"Greetings," Henry said, without enthusiasm.

Monk grinned at the red-headed disciple of gloom who had taken some part in nearly all their previous misfortunes.

"Henry, you're wearing a chain," Monk remarked.

" 'Tis thy fault!" Henry complained.

"Why, Henry!" Monk looked misunderstood.

Henry explained, "If thee had refrained from that last escape I would not be here."

"You mean you're in the chain gang because we escaped?"

"Verily."

"The last escape was a Jonah!" Monk sighed. "If we'd refrained, maybe we wouldn't be here, either."

"Oh, but thee would!" Henry said.

"Eh?"

" 'Twas planned from the first to put thee in chains."

Yanking on the sled had come to a halt while Doc and his two aids were being added to the chain gang. When one of the guards shouted, the yanking on the chain resumed.

Prince Albert, standing to one side, picked up a small rock and pegged it at Monk. "Get in there and pull, you baboon!"

Monk howled indignantly. He also jumped up and down and shook his chain.

Ham volunteered, "You look just like a big ape they keep chained in the Bronx zoo."

Monk ignored this insult and yelled, "Danged if I'm gonna pull rocks for anybody!"

"Neither am I!" Ham decided.

Doc Savage said, "It does seem something of an imposition."

Henry listened to this with interest, and sighed.

" 'Tis evident," Henry hazarded, "that thou art not going to work."

"Yea, verily," Monk growled.

" 'Tis a good idea," Henry said. He sat on the sled.

Inevitable complications arrived. Prince Albert threw other rocks—larger ones—at Monk, and the homely chemist threw them back with good aim; Monk also seized one of the stone blocks off the sled, a mass of rock weighing hundreds of pounds.

The squat, powerful chemist did a respectable job of heaving this stone at a fellow who was trying to prod him with a lance, after which the guards charged, having prudently discarded lances and swords which could be seized and used against them. It took about five minutes to overcome Doc Savage and the others.

"Throw 'em back into the sand pit," Prince Albert ordered. "We'll take the juice out of 'em!!"

The "sand pit" turned out to be the stone cistern in which they had been confined earlier. Hardly had they landed in it— Henry being hurled in along with them—when sand began sifting down on them.

Doc Savage said, "We had best get organized with the funnel. If we let the sand fill the place, we'll suffocate."

They devoted about five minutes of frenzied search for the funnel in the sand, but did not locate it.

"They took the darned funnel!" Monk gasped.

They found the small aperture in the wall and poured several handfuls of sand into it, then made another unpleasant discovery:

The hole had been blocked!

Monk squeaked, "This is gonna be something!"

Doc and his group stood in startled silence: the situation seemed infinitely blacker than a moment before, for the sand sifted down steadily from the hole in the ceiling—powder-fine stuff that saturated the air. They could not help breathing it.

"I think the stuff is comin' in faster than before!" Monk began to cough.

" 'Twas a sad day when I met thee," Henry complained.

"Henry," Doc said, "what do you think they will do to us?"

"Naught that is pleasant."

"The Duchess Portia is the mind behind this?" Doc demanded.

"Aye. She fooled thee in New York." Henry groaned feelingly. "We had a measure of peace before she and her vassal came to this island."

"Vassal? Who do you mean?"

"Prince Albert," Henry explained.

"I agree with the vassal part!" Monk grunted.

The men tore strips off their nightgownlike garments and tied these over their mouths and nostrils.

Doc Savage said, "Henry, there is a great deal about this that has us puzzled. Just what was the situation on the island before the Duchess Portia came?"

"Peace reigned," Henry said, and sighed.

"I mean—how many people were on the island in the beginning?"

"Two hundred or thereabouts," Henry replied.

Monk interrupted, "Do they all talk like you do?"

"Not all," Henry admitted.

"What we're getting at, Henry," Doc Savage said patiently, "is how you and two hundred others like you happened to be on this island."

"Generations ago we came from England," Henry explained.

Henry was no fountain of information; he did not flow, but had to be pumped, and Doc, Monk and Ham took turns at the pumping. What they learned was somehow not as dramatic as they had expected.

THE island was named King John Island, and it was located in the remote south Atlantic and had been colonized two or three centuries ago by Englishmen. Existence of the place was not unknown to geographers and historians.

It was simply that the island was unhandy for ships, produced no raw material of trade value, and was so remotely located that ships rarely stopped at the place. Just an island that had been colonized and forgotten.

"There are several such islands scattered over the globe," Doc Savage said. "You rarely hear of them."

Doc and his aids managed to learn from Henry that Duchess Portia Montanye-Norwich had arrived at the island aboard a yacht. There had been a disgruntled faction on the island, a group dissatisfied with such a hermit existence.

Some of these fellows had left the island on previous occasions, but without money, and confronted by the customs of a strange civilization, they had come back, defeated, to the island.

To these dissatisfied ones, Portia had presented an inviting prospect: piracy! She would supply a submarine if the islanders would operate it. Portia had explained about the European nations being at loggerheads with each other, so that submarine piracy was practical.

"But the men on the chain gang," Doc Savage said. "Who were they?"

"They are islanders who are being punished for not submitting to the pirates."

"Then there are other people on the island who are not pirates?"

"Aye," Henry nodded.

"Would they help us fight the pirates?"

"They would be afraid."

By now, the filtering sand was above their waists. Ham, floundering around, bogged down in the stuff, got it into his mouth and nostrils, and began to gag.

"Take it easy," Doc advised.

The bronze man removed his gown, ripped it up the back, then spread it out on the sand, and managed by careful maneuvering to roll on to it. The others followed this example; by shifting the gowns from time to time, they managed to keep on top of the sand.

Overhead, the guard seemed unpleasantly interested in their comfort, for several times he poked a flashlight beam down through the trapdoor bars, and on each occasion gave a satisfied grunt.

Doc Savage shoved one corner of his robe under the sand, so the ripping noise would be inaudible, and tore off a yard-square piece. With great pains, he loaded this with sand, then tied it, making a ball of a size halfway between a baseball and a football.

Henry began, "What——"

Doc got hold of Henry's shoulder and exerted enough pressure to emphasize necessity for silence.

Next, the bronze man stretched Monk and Ham out directly below the iron-grilled trapdoor, then he managed to stand on their backs, from which foundation, he could reach the trapdoor bars.

Doc Savage took his time tensing his throat muscles, setting his vocal chords—he was skilled at voice imitation, but this was no time for failure. He waited until he had extracted from his trained memory many characteristics of Prince Albert's voice.

And when Doc spoke, projecting his voice through the grating, he added just another ventriloquial effect so that the guard could not locate the source of the voice.

The bronze man managed to imitate Prince Albert's harsh tones with fantastic exactness.

"Open the trapdoor!" Doc shouted. "We've got another guy to throw in the sand pit!"

Doc Savage, face close to the grating, saw the guard start and stare toward the door. The guard was puzzled.

"Open the pit, you dumb cluck!" Doc said, using Prince Albert's snarl.

The slow-witted guard reached down, unfastened the trapdoor and yanked it open. As a precaution, he looked into the pit.

Doc Savage hit him between the eyes with the sandbag he had made out of his nightgown garment.

As the guard toppled into the hole, Monk grabbed the fellow and tried to wallop him one on the chance that he was still conscious. As a result of his activity, Monk sank into the sand, and grabbed Ham as a life preserver. There was a distressed flurry which did not subside until Doc hauled all of them out of the pit.

"You ignutz!" Ham hissed at Monk.

"Forsooth!" Henry said gloomily. "Now they will feed us all to the hounds!"

There was gloom through the castle, and silence, except for an occasional footstep or a voice. There was a trace of cooking smells in the air.

"Must be about noon," Monk decided.

Doc Savage indicated a barred window at the end of a passage, through which showed a fragment of gaudy sunset.

"On the contrary," he said, "it seems to be evening."

"The dogs," Henry muttered gloomily, "are kept half starved. They are always with appetite."

"We can't stand around and talk," Ham said practically.

Monk remarked, embarrassed, "Has anybody noticed that we're naked as little babes?"

Doc Savage moved down the corridor and took a cautious look around a corner, saw no one, and went on. The others followed. As Ham had said, they could not stand around and talk. Outside, there was still too much light to think of escaping unobserved from this castlelike building on the top of a rocky peak.

Being reluctant to explore when there was so much chance of discovery, the bronze man remained in the part of the stone building that he knew.

Since Doc and his group needed a hiding place, they investigated what was behind each door; the first half a dozen rooms held nothing but medieval furniture. Then, unexpectedly, they made a discovery. Doc Savage pointed.

"Our equipment!" Ham breathed ecstatically.

The room was not large. The floor was littered with stuff which had evidently come from New York on the submarine: bundles of newspapers, stacks of magazines, cases of liquor and cardboard boxes from ready-to-wear establishments.

Particularly interesting was the clothing which had been taken from Doc Savage and his men. The stuff lay on a box. It included the bronze man's gadget vest. They went into the room and dressed with haste. Doc put on the vest.

"I'm beginning to feel better," Monk grinned.

Chapter XV

THE TERRIBLE ISLAND

HENRY had been searching the cardboard boxes for garb for himself. The only articles he could find were trousers and coat, and without shirt or shoes, his angular red-headed figure presented a ludicrous picture.

Doc Savage investigated a door at the far side of the room, found it unlocked, and shoved it open. It gave into a room carpeted in mauve and equipped with bedroom furniture. The windows had iron bars outside, and were also fitted with Venetian blinds and attractive curtains. There were several doors; with one exception, these admitted to closets, and the remaining door gave into a richly furnished parlor.

In the closets were feminine garments, among which was the white regalia which had been worn during the morning by the Duchess Portia.

The bronze man indicated a closet which held feminine outdoor garments. It was not likely this closet would be visited this late in the evening, and it was large.

"Here is where we hide out," the bronze man announced.

"In the lady's boudoir!" Monk muttered. "I hope nobody hears about this."

They got into the closet and closed the door, then worked around behind the female garments and sat down. It was intensely dark.

Doc Savage fished in his vest and located the little padded metal case which held his glass anæsthetic grenades. He removed one grenade, held his breath and broke the grenade with his fingers.

Doc continued to hold his breath until regular deep breathing of his three companions indicated they had been overcome by the anæsthetic gas.

Still holding his breath, Doc got out of the closet and went

85

to the bedroom window which was open. The anæsthetic gas was odorless, colorless; tricky stuff that would knock a man out before there was a possibility of detecting it.

After he filled his lungs with fresh air coming in the window, Doc went back and closed the closet door on the three sleeping men, then made sure there was enough of a crack at the bottom of the door to give them air.

He left the bedroom.

Doc used more speed than caution. The cooking odors in the huge stone building indicated occupants might be at dinner, and he was taking a chance on that. His guess was evidently good, because he reached the gate without encountering any one. A guard stood outside the gate; he was astride his lance, like a witch on a broomstick, holding it with his knees while he swiped the blade with a whetstone.

Doc Savage came up behind the guard silently, got one arm around the fellow's head to cover his eyes, banded the fellow's chest with the other arm.

Then Doc rasped orders at imaginary companions.

"Monk!" he said. "Knock him out! Ham, Henry—run down the path! Get the drawbridge guard!"

Hoping he had planted the idea that Monk, Ham and Henry were with him, Doc landed a fist on the guard's jaw hard enough to make the man unconscious.

The bronze man dropped the guard and ran down the path. There was a strong wind blowing.

THE bronze man turned as he ran to look back at the huge stone building. It loomed like a castle, huge and cold in the moonlight.

If there was another watchman, it would defeat Doc's plan to give the impression that all the prisoners had fled the castlelike building. But there must have been no other sentinel, and no one watching the path from the windows, for there was no alarm.

The castle—it was more like a castle than anything else—stood squarely on the rocky stone peak, and apparently could be reached only by this one path which was cut in the sheer stone. The bronze man ran easily, his metallic features showing some concern, for there was still the drawbridge and its attendant.

Nearing the drawbridge, Doc slowed and kept close to the

face of the cliff; he began using the little mirror arrangement he employed as a periscope.

Four men attended the drawbridge, so evidently this was the vital spot of the castle's isolation. The guards were alert. Two stood watching down the path. Two stood facing the direction of the castle.

Doc Savage used care that a flash of his periscope mirror did not betray his presence. Drawbridge and guards were over a hundred feet away. There seemed no chance whatever of his approaching unobserved.

After he had debated ways and means, Doc removed two grenade cases from the vest, and from one of these extracted a little metal egg, heavy for its size. Tripping the firing lever of this, he pegged it out over the path edge into space. The time it took to fall gave an unpleasant idea of the cliff's height.

The report was riflelike. The whole cliff seemed to jump a little. A few loose rocks cascaded. The drawbridge guards jumped to the path rim and looked down to see what had happened.

Doc Savage ran toward the guards. He got up on his toes, went as quietly as he could. He watched the guards; when he saw that the grenade explosion was not going to hold their attention until he reached them, he pegged two grenades from the second case.

These eggs were smokers, which stopped rolling near the guards and erupted enormous wads of black smoke. The astounded guards yelled, floundered in the sepia vapor. Doc Savage got into the smoke with them. He had to work fast because of the wind.

"Monk!" he yelled. "Ham! Henry! Work fast!"

There was a volley of blows and grunting as two of the guards made a mistake and started fighting each other.

The night before, the bronze man had secured an idea of the drawbridge's mechanism. The ponderous span was lifted by a man-power windlass, and the windlass was locked by looping a rope over one of the handles.

Doc yanked the rope loop off the handle; chains snarled, clumsy mechanism squealed, and the heavy drawbridge came down with a crash.

"Come on!" Doc Savage shouted.

He ran across the drawbridge, making enough stamping to sound like four men, and went on down the cliff path. To keep the guards from learning that he was one man and not four, he left several smoke bombs to hatch on the path. The wind made the stuff boil, carried it away quickly. But it served its purpose.

MUCH of the bronze man's past success was due to his methods, to his habit of doing the unexpected; he avoided making a direct approach to any obvious goal, for the reason that as long as he did not do what an enemy thought he would do, the enemy was likely to be confused and less able to cause trouble.

At the present time, the obvious course, now that he and his men had escaped, would be flight from the castle and then from the island. But he had no immediate intention of doing either.

His men were still in the castle, probably in the safest possible spot, now that he had created the impression that they were not there. Instead of fleeing from the island, Doc intended to investigate the people who were on it.

The inhabitants of the island interested him. Other people's misfortune was the bronze man's business. This island itself was like any other rocky island, hence not particularly interesting. The inhabitants of the place, while unusual, were not unique, there being other islands in the world inhabited by strange people.

The predicament of these particular islanders was both remarkable and terrible. That part of them should turn pirates was startling. That this group should enslave the others was unpleasant. From what Doc Savage had seen, the enslavement might be pretty hideous.

A survey of the island situation was his immediate object. It might be possible to organize resistance.

Doc reached the foot of the cliff. The path went on to the bay, and he followed it, although the bay was not his destination. The sun was just about gone, its departure smearing rusty luminance over the bleak stone and impoverished shrubbery.

Evidently the inhabited portion of the island was a plateau commencing about half a mile from the castle, and spreading over the central portion of the island. A number of stone structures, hard to distinguish in the moonlight, but probably a village, stood approximately a mile from the foot of the cliff.

Doc quit the path and entered thick brush. He went far enough to give the impression that he had entered the brush to get concealment, still going toward the tiny bay.

He traveled rapidly, watching the ground; when he came to a sandy spot that would take footprints, he doubled over, and with his hands, made imitation tracks of three other men in the sand with his own. This to further convince pursuers— there was sure to be pursuit—that all the prisoners had escaped the castle.

A hundred yards farther on, the bronze man took care of the hounds. He did this by sprinkling his trail with a bilious-looking, weird-smelling liquid from a tiny phial. A great deal of experimenting had gone into the concoction of that malodorous liquid.

Almost every animal has some particular scent which arouses its fear; lion smell, for instance, terrifies horses; sharks are driven to mad fear by the presence of certain poisonous seaweeds; and this liquid was a combination of all these terrifying scents that was possible to assemble. Doc Savage had used it to frighten off sharks, and it would send the dogs away yelping in apprehension.

Having made a plain trail, then ended it, Doc Savage headed for his real destination: the homes of the unfortunate islanders. The gale beat at him and he could hear the moan and pound of the wind-tormented sea.

THE huts were of stone, with thatched roofs. Huts exactly like them can be seen by thousands along the English country-side, some three years old, some three hundred, the English small house apparently being an architectural type perpetually popular.

It was dark when Doc Savage reached the village. There were a few clouds now, scudding before the wind, but when-ever there were no clouds, the moon was pouring an incon-venient amount of silver light.

The village houses were arrayed along a single road, which was edged with low stone walls. The bronze man got close to one wall and listened.

In a very few moments, he was aware of something un-natural about the village; at first, he failed to understand exactly what it was. There was light in the houses. Smoke climbed from most of the chimneys. Pigs, sheep and goats roamed about, and there were a few cows.

It was a peaceful enough rural scene to the eye, but there was something unhappy about it. Something depressing. Suddenly, Doc Savage got it—the silence! There should have been noise in the houses, and laughter, but there was none. Just an ill-omened hush.

The bronze man started to leave his shelter, changed his mind upon hearing hoofbeats. Horses were approaching the village from the direction of the castle. Three horsemen, apparently. In a few moments, they clattered past, big dark horses and squat, powerful men wearing armor and carrying lances, and entered the village.

The horsemen had a grim air of having an errand to do.

Curious, Doc Savage drifted along the stone fence after the riders. Enough shadow banked the wall so that there was very little chance of his being discovered.

The horsemen reined up before one of the more miserable huts. They dismounted.

"Open up, Rowe!" one bellowed.

Without waiting for a response, he kicked the rickety door off its hinges.

The three horsemen stamped inside, and as they passed through the light from the wrecked door, Doc Savage saw that they were burly men, and bearded.

Doc Savage moved near enough so that the horses caught his presence and blew nervously. He could hear all that was said in the house.

The man who had kicked down the door was roaring.

"Where'd the prisoners go?" he yelled.

The answer was given by a middle-aged voice that was highly nervous—obviously Rowe.

"I haven't—haven't seen them," Rowe quavered.

The questioner did not pursue that point; evidently his mission was not to find Doc and the others.

"Rowe, thou turned in but half thy quota of barley to-day!" the man shouted. "What about that?"

"I—I had to leave the field at noon," Rowe quavered.

Rowe was scared.

"Damn you, Rowe!" bellowed the other. "Thou knowest the quota! Thou knowest we need that grain to provision the submarines."

"I had to quit at noon!" Rowe said wildly.

The other swore. "And why did thee have to quit?"

"I had to take care of my boy," Rowe explained nervously. "The kid is sick."

"Thou knowest the orders about getting in that barley?" the other demanded sharply.

"Yes. But——"

"Get the kid out in the road!" the ugly-voiced horseman bellowed.

"Wait a minute!" Rowe yelled. "What are you——"

There was a whistle, followed by a meaty sound, evidently made by a whip. Rowe screeched in agony. There was scuffling. A woman screamed. A childish voice cried out feebly. Then the three horsemen came dragging a boy into the road.

THE boy was seven or eight and looked fragile for his age. He was, Doc Savage perceived at once, suffering from one of the worse stages of pneumonia. He breathed with great difficulty, and lacked strength to stand when the big, bearded men pitched him into the road.

One of the horsemen carried a kerosene lamp out of the house and hurled it at the thatched roof. The lamp broke, sprayed oil, and flames instantly bundled the roof.

Another of the riders had a whip, an ugly thing with a long, loaded handle tipped with several heavy wires about two feet long and with common iron taps tied to their ends.

"Beat the kid!" the spokesman ordered.

Rowe dashed forward, yelling incoherently. The spokesman swung a lance hat against the side of his head. Rowe fell down and squirmed a little.

"We beat you before, and it did no good," the spokesman growled. "Methinks the lash on the boy might have more effect on thee."

The whip hissed a little going through the air, and when it hit the boy, all his muscles seemed to jerk at once.

The spokesman lifted the whip, and when his arm got to the top of its upswing, the whip left his hand and sailed away, turning over and over, its lashes distended like an octopus's tentacles.

The whip wielder made a noise, a kind of gurgle. His lower face would probably never look quite the same again, for Doc Savage had hit him hard enough to break the jaw in too many places for it to ever mend in a proper shape.

Doc Savage hit the man again, in the middle this time, then gave attention to the spokesman. The latter howled, jabbed with his lance.

Doc avoided the lance point, got in, and broke several ribs, then knocked the man backward a dozen feet with a blow to the jaw.

The third horseman had a pistol. He tried to get it. It was one of the big horse pistols, and the man got it out just as Doc got hold of his arms. They fell down, and there were some bone-breaking noises, a strangled scream, and silence.

The bronze man got up, realizing for the first time that he had lost his temper.

Chapter XVI

THE FIGHT

PEOPLE stood in the street now. They had come from their houses, and they were dejected, terrified-looking people; they looked as though the spirit had been whipped out of them, and they seemed aghast at what had happened. There was no disapproval. But there was terror of consequences.

The blazing roof of Rowe's house cast a lurid hell-light over their tyrannized faces.

"Get buckets and water!" Doc Savage said sharply. "Put out that fire!"

They jumped at his voice, like people who were used to jumping. Some of them ran for water.

Doc Savage picked up the sick boy and carried him across the street and into a house. The ill child's mother, a thin woman with a face that was a map of fear, followed. Rowe got up and followed, also. He staggered and bled, but he was more worried about his son than anything else.

"Hot water," Doc Savage said.

He put the sick boy on a rickety bed in a miserable room that had nothing to recommend it except cleanliness. He tapped the child's chest, listened, tapped some more. The pneumonia was in both lobes.

The bronze man got a phial of small pellets out of his vest. He poured half of these in the hand of the sick boy's mother.

"Wet them," he ordered, "and see that the boy breathes the fumes. The pellets will slowly turn into gas."

The mother looked blank, uncomprehending.

Doc Savage explained, "They are a concentrated chemical which has exactly the same effect on the human system as oxygen. We hold one of those in our mouth, and go under water and stay down for long periods. That is what we used

93

them for. This boy needs oxygen. We haven't any, and those pellets are the next best thing. You understand?"

The mother nodded, but remained wordless.

Doc Savage said to Rowe, "Come outside."

Rowe followed him out, clutched the bronze man and gasped, "What's the kid's chances?"

"Fair," the bronze man said.

Rowe shook a little, and made some kind of sound that might mean anything, but obviously meant relief.

Across the street, a bucket brigade was putting water on the burning roof. They had it about extinguished.

The three horsemen lay where they had fallen. They would lay their quite a while, unless some one moved them.

Doc asked, "You have to put up with this sort of thing?"

"What can we do?" Rowe set his teeth in his lips.

Doc Savage pointed at the senseless horsemen. "They have bones that will break, just as you and I."

"Yes," Rowe admitted. "But there's a lot of them, and a lot of guns, and the dogs. Don't forget those dogs. They ride patrol with them all night every night. And if those dogs catch a man——" He shuddered so violently that Doc Savage put a supporting hand on his arm.

Doc said, "You seem to speak a fairly decent brand of English."

"Most of us do," Rowe said.

"Those in the castle do not."

"They're the ignorant element," Rowe explained grimly. "They were the first to fall in with this devilish thing."

"What about the one called Prince Albert?"

"He is not a native. He came to this island when—when this all began."

"And Henry?"

Rowe frowned, puzzled. "A lot of us are named Henry. It is a popular name. I do not know which one you mean."

Doc Savage let Henry drop.

"What about the Duchess Portia?" Doc asked.

Rowe spat.

"That woman," he muttered, "is the devil in skirts! She is responsible for all this!"

THE fire was out now. And the fire fighters, still holding their buckets, gathered around Doc Savage and Rowe. The other people of the village came and joined them, and they formed a circle, a silent, staring ring. No word was said for minutes.

Then, "You'd better run for it!" a man told Doc Savage hoarsely.

Rowe gripped Doc Savage's arm. "He's right. They'll come to see what happened to the three you overpowered. And they'll bring the dogs."

The whole ring of staring, pale faces nodded frightened agreement.

"Will they do anything to you?" Doc Savage asked.

There was silence.

"Will they?" the bronze man asked sharply.

"They will beat some of us," Rowe admitted.

"And you'll stand for it?" Doc demanded.

Rowe swallowed. "Yes," he said.

"Why?"

Rowe took a tight grip with his fingers on the bronze man's arms. "You don't get this," he said hoarsely. "We didn't take this lying down. We fought them, at first. But they've got guns, and those dogs. And they outnumber us two to one. We can't do anything."

The ring of faces nodded miserable agreement.

"We can do nothing," a man said. "We know that now."

Another man said, "Some day, when they have looted enough off ships, and have enough treasure, they will go away."

The last statement was nothing more or less than a voice of desperate hope.

Doc Savage looked at them, his flake gold eyes moving from one to the other, studying, plumbing their dejection, measuring the degree to which they had surrendered to fatalism.

He asked, "What about ships? Surely ships come to this place?"

"Two have come," Rowe admitted. "They were simply told there was no trading to be had, and given fresh water. They went away."

Doc Savage finished his inspection of the faces.

"Have you any idea who I am?" he asked.

Rowe said, "We heard they brought back four prisoners. Three men and a woman. You must be one of the prisoners."

"My name," Doc said, "is Doc Savage."

The name apparently did not mean a thing to Rowe, and that was unfortunate. Most of the time Doc Savage preferred anonymity; he drew a great deal of embarrassment from the fact that his name, his reputation, had spread to the corners of the earth and he could, by merely appearing on the streets of almost any large city, collect a crowd of fans and autograph hounds.

This was one exception. He wished these people knew him. It would take a strong magnet to draw them together in a group that would fight.

Doc Savage studied the ring of faces. They were cowed, of course, and fearful, but these people had been born on this rugged island, had grown up amid elemental closeness to nature and they must have fighting spirit, on the theory that the most indefatigable battler is an aborigine out of a primitive jungle.

"If you had guns," Doc Savage said quietly, "would it make a difference?"

Rowe wet his lips with the tip of his tongue and did not answer immediately. Several of the bystanders drew closer and began to hold their jaws in a way which made their faces look more like the faces of men.

Finally, "You got guns?" Rowe asked.

"We might get them," Doc said.

"You can't get them," Rowe shook his head. "If you had the guns, it might be different."

Doc Savage decided to stop wishing that these people knew more about him so that they would have more confidence in his ability to get guns.

"There's the dogs," Rowe muttered.

"The dogs won't bother us," Doc said.

"They will eat a man alive!" Rowe muttered.

Doc Savage decided against explaining his chemical concoction which was a defense against the big canines. The stuff was somewhat fantastic; if he started telling these people about such a liquid, they might get the idea he was crazy. He did not want to undermine their confidence.

The bronze man decided to use harsh arguments. It might help if he struck grim blows in trying to mold their decision to help him.

"Rowe," Doc said, "they will kill you!"

"But——"

"The three horsemen were at your house when they were overpowered," Doc Savage said. "When a party from the castle comes to punish the village, they will make an example of you."

Rowe changed from one foot to the other. Obviously, he was convinced that was exactly what would happen.

"They will beat your boy!" Doc Savage continued. "And it is absolutely certain that another beating will kill him."

"I guess you're right," Rowe said hollowly. "I'm with you. But what can we do?"

"We need one other man," Doc Savage said. "He must be stocky and wide-shouldered."

Promptly, a man shouldered out of the circle of villagers. He was certainly stocky enough; he looked sufficiently powerful to give Monk a tussle. He also had an impressive quantity of bristling black beard.

"I'm in this, gov'nor!" he growled.

"You'll do excellently," Doc said. "We will not have to put a beard on you."

"Beard?"

"The three of us are going to make up as the three horsemen," Doc Savage explained.

THE job of masquerading as the three horsemen went farther than putting on the garments and armor which the trio of riders had worn. There was a matter of beards. All three of the horsemen had prolific whiskers, whereas Doc Savage and Rowe were clean-shaven.

Rowe had a razor, however, one somewhat ineffective because the blade had been broken down to a length of hardly more than an inch to prevent its use as a weapon; the pirates had done that. Doc managed to shave the three senseless horsemen and got enough whiskers to make scraggly beards for himself and Rowe.

They stuck the hair on with resinous gum which some one went out and scraped off a scrubby evergreen tree, a glue substitute that was not very effective, since patches of whiskers came off at the slightest excuse. However, it was the only thing available.

The three horsemen were bound and concealed under the floor of Rowe's house.

Doc Savage, Rowe and the third man mounted the horses. They looked vaguely like the men they were impersonating. They galloped toward the castle, the armor clanking and gouging them, the lances bouncing around, and parts of their beards in imminent danger of blowing away.

The gale was so cold it needled them, and the sky had somewhat an aspect of blued-steel, with stars as cold-looking as snow flakes.

"The dogs!" Rowe croaked suddenly.

Clamor of the pack blasted down from the cliff path. Doc Savage knew that his trail was being followed. Listening, he caught the noise of horsemen following the dogs, the yelling of the riders. The hound pack came down the cliff path with astonishing speed.

"We'd better pull up for a while," Doc Savage said.

The three of them stopped, and Rowe muttered, "Are the dogs on your trail?"

Doc Savage admitted that they were, but did not add that he wanted to be sure the chemical mixture that he had sprayed on his back trail would be effective.

They sat on the horses and waited for what seemed a long time. Then baying of the dog pack stopped. Eerie stillness ensued. A dog yelped in terror; the whole pack could be heard piling back toward the castle.

"The dogs—they're scared!" Rowe gasped.

"The stuff worked," Doc said.

"What caused it?"

Doc Savage explained about the chemical. He told it quietly, convincingly, and managed to make his two listeners accept it as something perfectly logical.

They rode onto the cliff path, all three abreast, then climbed it and approached the drawbridge.

"Make the horses prance," Doc Savage suggested. "That will take attention from ourselves."

They rode up to the end of the drawbridge gap. Doc Savage aped the voice of the horseman who had beaten the boy.

"Let that thing down!" Doc bellowed.

The guards on the other side of the bridge swore at him,

then lowered the span. Doc and his two companions rode across. They made their horses prance by using reins and heels.

"The prisoners haven't been caught!" shouted one of the bridge guards. He was deceived as to their identity.

" 'Twas the dogs after the captives that we heard, eh?" Doc growled.

"Aye!"

"But the dogs quit!"

The bridge guard cursed and said something about that being the dangdest kind of mystery, much of what he said being lost as Doc Savage and the other two drove their horses up the part of the trail which was a flight of steps.

Reaching the castle gate, they spurred their horses straight through.

There was a new guard at the gate, and he shouted a demand for news of the escaped prisoners.

"They are probably not far away," Doc Savage said.

Chapter XVII

UNLUCKY PLANE

Rowe knew the castle layout, and he whispered that the stables were to the left, so they rode in that direction. There were no attendants around, and they dismounted and tied the horses in the stalls with knots that could be quickly undone. The principal lighting system of the castle consisted of old-fashioned tallow candles which shed negligible light.

Depending on the gloom and their own boldness to throw suspicion from themselves, Doc Savage and the other two went directly to Portia's bedchamber. The room was unoccupied. They went in silently, and Doc Savage opened the closet door. Monk, Ham and Henry still slept inside.

Doc Savage grabbed the slumbering trio out, and administered stimulants which gradually overcame the effects of the gas.

Monk opened his eyes, peered at Doc Savage and blinked. "Dang it, Doc," he mumbled, "you must've broke one of them anæsthetic eggs by mistake." Then he caught sight of Rowe and the other man. *"What the blazes!"*

"Not too loud!" Doc warned.

Ham got his wits organized and asked, "What happened, Doc?"

"We're going to work on this," Doc explained.

"But why make us unconscious?" Ham demanded. "What was the idea of that?"

When Doc Savage seemed not to hear the question, Ham did not repeat the inquiry, having learned from experience that when Doc ignored a question put as plainly as that one, there was no use repeating it.

Henry made muttering noises, rubbed his jaw, scratched his head, and looked bewildered.

Rowe scowled at Henry. "I've seen this man with the pirates!" he growled. "I think he——"

"Never mind," Doc Savage interrupted. "Henry is being useful to us. We won't discuss him."

"What happens next?" Monk wanted to know.

Doc Savage moved around the bedroom scrutinizing the place. Cleansing creams, lotions and powder on the dressing table were modern enough. Articles had been moved since he was last here. In the wastebasket, he found freshly used cleansing tissue which indicated that Portia had been in the bedroom during his absence.

Doc confronted Henry. "Where is China's room?"

"China?" Henry looked puzzled.

"The new girl prisoner," Doc explained.

Henry pointed to a door. "In there—another bedroom."

Doc Savage went to the door, found it would open silently, got it ajar, and put his head inside. He stepped into another bedroom longer than the one he had just left and not nearly as wide.

China stood at the window at the far end. Her elbows were propped on the stone window sill. She wore a loose-flowing gown of black, caught at the waist with black cord. She made a tall and nunlike figure, except for the striking contrast of her bright honey-blond hair.

Doc Savage went silently to China, clasped a hand over her mouth and held her. It was probably a good thing the hand was over her mouth, or the scream she tried to get out would have removed part of the roof. Doc Savage let her see who he was, then released her.

"You'll be the death of me yet!" China gasped. "You couldn't have said, 'Hello,' or something?"

"*Sh-h-h!*" Doc requested.

He led China into the next room, and the young woman stared at the other men. The fact that there were six, including Doc, plainly surprised her.

"You've been collecting!" she remarked.

Monk sidled up to Doc. Monk had a grip on Henry's arm. "Doc!" Monk whispered. "I think Henry's got something!"

"Eh?" Doc said.

"Henry says they've got a plane here," Monk explained. "It's a seaplane."

Doc Savage said, "They have collapsible planes on the submarines. But none of those ships are big enough to take us away from here."

"This is a big plane," Monk declared. "They use it to make daily flights to spot any steamers that might be near the island."

"Where is it?"

"In a hangar on the shore of the bay, Henry says."

Doc Savage eyed Henry. "Do they keep a guard over this plane?"

"Aye," Henry admitted. "But only two men."

"And you think we could get it?"

"Aye."

"Then," Doc Savage said, "we'll take the plane."

HENRY seemed much pleased. He beamed, rubbed his hands and immediately volunteered to be of further help.

"I know a secret route to the stables," he announced. "Methinks 'twould help if I ventured ahead and saddled mounts for all."

It surprised Monk and Ham to hear Doc Savage's low, trilling note, the small, unconscious thing which he did in moments of mental stress, come into being for a brief moment.

"Go ahead and saddle the horses," the bronze man directed.

Henry nodded, went to the door, listened, and stepped outside. He went down the corridor toward the stables, but instead of going to the stables, he turned sharply to the right.

He had not covered a score of yards, when he met Prince Albert, who immediately grabbed Henry and scowled.

"How long is this act of yours gonna go on?" Prince Albert snarled.

"It was my plan," Henry said dryly. "Thou promised to let me give the orders for the time being."

"If you've got some orders, give 'em!" Prince Albert growled. "It's about time!"

"Ye will order every one to keep out of this part of the castle," Henry commanded, with the gusto of a corporal telling his general what to do.

"But——"

"And keep clear of the route to the stables," Henry added.

"Well, I'll be——"

"Do so at once!" Henry commanded sharply.

Prince Albert scratched his bullet of a head wonderingly and obeyed. It did not take long to get loiterers out of that part of the castle. Henry and Prince Albert retired to a room for a conference.

"Send a man," Henry ordered, "to the stable. Have him saddle seven horses."

Prince Albert took care of that, then came back and peered at Henry. "I don't get this."

"They plan to escape in a plane," Henry explained.

"But——"

" 'Twas neat work on my part that arranged it." Henry grinned.

"Hell!" Prince Albert complained. "I thought you was gonna find out if they left any word back in New York that was gonna give us trouble?"

Henry's grin widened. "I did that."

"How?"

" 'Twas easy. I did but ask the homely one, Monk, if there was chance of Doc Savage getting help from the outside. Monk said no one knew they were here, and that none knew aught of this island."

Prince Albert let out a relieved breath. "That's swell!"

" 'Tis that."

"But," Prince Albert grunted, "after you learned that, I thought we were just gonna put them out of the way."

"We are," Henry explained. "You will go at once to the plane, draw gas from the tanks, shut off the fuel lines, and fill the tanks with water."

"Now what——"

"There will be enough fuel in the tanks to let them take off. The water will make the fuel gauges read full. They will not be suspicious. They will crash."

"What you mean is they'll land on the sea and we'll have to fight 'em all over again."

"Listen," Henry said.

They stood silent. Outside, the wind whooped and moaned and made banshee noises.

"In a sea such as yon wind is kicking up," Henry admitted, "we do not have to worry."

Prince Albert rubbed his jaw. "Still, that plane cost dough."

"The plane is a cheap price," Henry said. "Doc Savage hath incredible gadgets. I am not even sure that we could get rid of him and his men if we tried by violence."

"You're the boss," Prince Albert grunted.

Henry went back and joined Doc Savage and the others.

"The horses," Henry said innocently, "are saddled."

ALL took off their shoes in order to move more quietly and gathered at the door and waited for instructions. Monk and Ham had taken charge of the attractive China; Rowe and the other man from the village were frankly scared. Doc Savage made a slight gesture. They started through the door.

Then a new voice gasped, "Just a minute!"

They turned and stared at the speaker.

It was the Duchess Portia Montanye-Norwich, and she stood just inside the other door, gazing at them in wide-eyed amazement.

Henry muttered something guttural.

Suddenly, Portia came toward them. She walked steadily, as if not afraid. There was anxiety rather than amazement on her face, appeal rather than accusation. She held one hand out slightly.

"You are escaping?" she breathed.

"That is the general idea," Doc Savage admitted.

Portia said, "Take me with you!" hoarsely.

Monk could not keep back a startled noise. "Take you?" the homely chemist gulped. "But you run this shebang!"

Portia shook her head. "I know what you think. But it's all wrong!"

Monk muttered, "But we saw you when——"

"You saw me doing only what they made me do!" Portia said. Her voice was low and frantic. "They've been using me as a front! You've got to believe that!"

To the utter astonishment of the entire group, probably most to the amazement of Monk and Ham, who knew him best, Doc Savage accepted Portia's statement at face value.

"Come on," he said. "We have no time to waste."

"But, Doc!" Ham exploded. "This woman is a bang-up liar! She fooled us to a fare-you-well in New York!"

"She's tryin' to fool us again!" Monk added.

Portia turned frantically to the long, blond showgirl, China.

"China," she said earnestly, "you know me! I had to deceive you, make you think my mind was behind all this. They threatened to kill you if I didn't. You've got to believe that!"

China bit her lips, examined her fingers, and showed plainly that she didn't know what to think. She stared at Doc Savage.

"I told you," China said, "that I always thought she was swell people. In New York, I thought she was on the level. She's a good actress. She could have fooled me here." China nipped her lips desperately. "And she could be fooling us right now, too!"

Doc Savage held to his earlier decision.

"Come on," he said.

They went with silent haste to the stable, meeting no one. While the others were getting on their horses, Doc Savage went ahead to the door.

The guard, as on the occasion of the bronze man's previous escape, was outside the door. It was not the same guard, and he was not sharpening his lance; that was the only difference.

He went down silently when Doc Savage took hold of him and put paralyzing pressure on his spinal nerve centers.

The bronze man went back to his party. They had saddled another horse for Portia. The whole group rode out of the castle gate and down the path, and there was no alarm given.

"Forsooth, we are very lucky," Henry said, as if he wanted them to understand there was nothing suspicious about their easy escape from the castle.

At the drawbridge, they had a fight. Doc Savage, Monk, Ham and Rowe rode ahead, spurring, and were upon the guards before they could organize really effective defense. Doc Savage and the others rode the guards down, then piled from saddles and used their fists. The fight lasted about thirty seconds.

"This is too dang easy!" Monk grumbled.

"Forsooth, we are lucky," Henry explained.

There was no sound from the castle, as if the drawbridge fight had not been heard. Doc Savage let the drawbridge down, then mounted and led his group on. Reaching the foot of the cliff, they spurred into a gallop.

Rowe reined his horse alongside Doc Savage.

"If we leave in the plane," he yelled, "what about the people in the village? We told them we would help them."

"We can come back," Doc explained.

Rowe considered that. Now that he had committed himself to resistance, he appeared to feel he might as well go whole hog all at once.

"I favor staying," he growled, "and fighting it out!"

Doc Savage did not comment. He called to Henry, asking whereabouts of the seaplane hangar.

" 'Tis yon way," Henry said, and pointed.

The bronze man gave Henry a sharp glance. Henry sounded extremely nervous.

"Something wrong?" Doc asked.

"I—uh—no," Henry gulped.

They rode on, circling the high rim of the bay, and reaching at last another path which led downward, this one at the far end of the bay.

The wind pushed against their faces, slapped loose parts of their clothing against their bodies. It made ghastly sounds in the crags through which they worked downward. They could hear the sea now. It was moaning and pounding.

"Some night," Monk complained.

At the bay shore, Henry indicated they should turn right.

"Around yon headland," he explained, "is the hangar."

The hangar was a structure of sheet metal over a steel framework, one of the knock-down type which can be shipped anywhere and erected.

It stood, not on the bay proper, but around the headland, as Henry had said, on a creek, where it was hidden from ships that might come into the bay. The seaplane simply taxied down the creek, around the headland and onto the bay whenever it took off.

"Henry," Doc Savage said, "there will be a guard, you believe?"

"Aye." Henry sounded even more scared.

"What's givin' you the jitters?" Monk asked him.

Henry did not answer. But his teeth chattered.

Doc Savage said, "Henry, you might come with me to get the guards. You know where they may be found."

Henry stopped rattling his teeth long enough to say, "Aye."

They had no more trouble with the hangar guards than with those at the drawbridge. There were two guards, and they were crouched just inside the hangar door, sheltered from the wind.

Imitating Prince Albert's voice, Doc Savage called, "Seen any sign of Doc Savage?"

The guards growled that they hadn't, and while they were growling, Doc Savage and Henry walked into the hangar and fell upon them. As soon as the fight started, Monk and the others came running. It was over when they got there.

Doc Savage turned his little flashlight on the plane. It was a modern ship, a big one. Ham swung into the cockpit, switched on instrument lights and examined the fuel gauges.

"Enough gas to make Africa," was his opinion.

"Get in the ship, all of you," Doc directed.

Henry's teeth chattering rose to a new high for volume.

Blonde China complained, "You sound like the accompaniment for a Cuban orchestra. What's eating you?"

Henry told what was eating him. He yelled it in a shrill, terror-stricken voice.

"I cuk-cuk-can't go with thee!" he screeched.

Monk gulped, "Huh?"

Henry, it seemed from his wailing, was afraid of planes.

THAT Henry should be afraid of a plane after what they had gone through struck Monk as ludicrous, and the homely chemist snorted mirthfully. That provoked Henry into a string of wild protestations. He thought of an assortment of reasons why he should not go along, and he told them all.

Henry would not be killed if he remained behind. He could help them when they returned to wipe out the pirates. He could work from the inside. He would die of fright if he went up in the plane; he just knew he would. He couldn't go. He couldn't!

Monk squeaked, "Doc, shall I give him an anæsthetic with my fist so he won't mind so much?"

"Let him stay," Doc Savage said.

"But——"

"He can be of marked help in wiping out the pirates later," Doc pointed out.

Henry was so relieved he gurgled. He jumped around delightedly, then helped them get chocks from in front of the wheels of the plane. He got behind and pushed after Doc

Savage started the two big plane motors and got the craft rolling into the water.

Henry even waded out to his armpits to help steer the craft. Then he stood and waved both arms in farewell until the plane was lost in the gloom beside the headland.

Then Henry began laughing. He laughed all the while he was wading out of the water and wringing out his clothes.

He chuckled while he trotted along the creek shore toward the bay. He could hear the plane's motors. The craft seemed to idle for a moment near the mouth of the creek, and Henry concluded the craft was getting a bearing on the submarine so as to miss it.

Henry snickered and put on more speed. He wanted to see the plane crash, or hear it.

He reached the bay shore in time to see the plane as a scudding black dot that sped across the bay, growing more and more vague in the moonlight, but lifting slowly off the water. The wind, fortunately, was coming straight in from the sea.

When the plane passed through the mouth of the bay, it was no more than two hundred feet above the water. Henry chuckled. Now if the motors just—just—and they did! They stopped. Both almost together.

The craft was low, and the crash into the sea followed almost immediately. The wind was loud, but the crash was louder. It was a very satisfactory crash.

Henry laughed until his sides began hurting, then he started back toward the castle.

Chapter XVIII

WAR ON AN ISLAND

HENRY's laughter was a little premature.

Monk, listening to it, had difficulty restraining himself. Ham, fathoming the impulse that was in the homely chemist's mind, took hold of Monk's ear and twisted it.

"You freak of nature!" Ham breathed. "Want to spoil Doc's plans?"

"I'd like to spoil that Henry!" Monk gritted.

Ham pointed out, "Henry is the lad that will make them think we're all finished. We want them to think that, so we can work without having everybody from the castle hunting us."

Doc Savage joined them at that point. All but the bronze man had piled out of the plane as it was rounding the headland; Doc had remained with the craft to lash the controls and see that it was going to take off, and had dived overboard before it got going too fast.

They listened to Henry go away laughing.

"When we clean house," Monk growled, "save Henry for me. He's my exclusive meat!"

Ham said, "Doc, how the blazes did you get wise to Henry?"

"It is a common practice for policemen to go into cells with criminals and pretend to be crooks," the bronze man explained. "When Henry joined us, it was a little too obvious. They were working the old police game on us. Watching Henry made it certain."

Monk snorted. He had remembered something.

"So that's why you gassed me and Ham and Henry while you went to the village," the homely chemist announced. "You didn't want Henry working any shenanigan, and at the same time you didn't want to make him suspicious."

Doc nodded.

Monk said, "Well, let's get organized. What do we do next?"

Doc Savage's voice was quiet. "Give them time to spread the word we are dead. They will call in their searching parties, and we'll have a clearer field."

The group found shelter from the cold wind and settled down to wait.

"We might as well get the situation here all clear in our minds," Doc Savage suggested. He addressed the Duchess Portia. "They used your money to buy the submarine and supplies, did they not?"

Portia gasped her astonishment. "You knew that?"

"It was a surmise," Doc explained. "The money from this had to come from somewhere. You are wealthy."

"I was," Portia admitted wryly. "I inherited a large fortune from my husband. But I suspect most of it is gone now."

"How did it start in the first place?" Doc inquired.

"Prince Albert," Portia said grimly. "After my husband's death, I suppose I went haywire. I got to hunting thrills, seeking interesting people. Prince Albert was interesting. He was a guest on my yacht, and he suggested we visit this island.

"When we got here, he had a gang on hand. They seized me. And from then on, they not only used my money, but made it appear I was the ringleader in the whole terrible thing."

Monk made a noise.

"I can't see," the homely chemist grumbled, "how they could make you kick in the dough."

Portia shuddered. "You have no idea what tortures they can use. You can be gotten into a state of mind, you know, where money doesn't seem so much, alongside other things. They used drugs, as well as—well—other things."

"What other things?" Monk wanted to know.

"Shut up, stupid!" Ham suggested.

But Portia explained. "They took one of my friends who was on the yacht, and poured molten lead into his ears. It is an old-fashioned torture, I understand. They made me watch it, until I fainted. My friend died."

"You don't need to describe any more," Monk mumbled. He put the end of a little finger in one of his ears gingerly.

"Prince Albert is the leader?" Doc asked.

"Yes. He's queer. He has to be a little crazy, you know, to do a thing like this. One of his fixations is to keep in the background. That is the strongest fixation."

"What's a fixation?" Monk demanded.

"Well, Prince Albert is always passing some one else off as the leader of the enterprise. He held me up as the leader. At one time, he intended to palm Doc Savage off on the world as the head of the submarine pirates, if anything went wrong. And at times, he uses Henry as the apparent head of things."

"Henry," Monk said, "is a gone gosling. Just wait'll I get hold of 'im!"

Doc Savage asked, "Just what happened to that submarine near Boston?"

Portia said, "They had taken me to the United States on that submarine because it was necessary for me to see my bankers personally before I could get money to pay for their second submarine—this one. They managed that by terrorizing me.

"Afterward, they put me on that other submarine, and we left Boston. I flooded the engine room with the oil, set fire to it and sprang overboard. I was rescued. Prince Albert, Henry and the others were already on shore because they had remained in New York to take delivery of the new submarine."

Portia took a deep, shaky breath. "I was terrified."

China came and put an arm around Portia. "Poor kid!" China said.

A FEW minutes later, the bronze man's party heard horses gallop down to the boat landing, and some one bellowed the tidings Doc Savage and the others were dead. The voice on the submarine howled back that the plane, having flown over the submarine before the crash, they should know it, shouldn't they?

The horsemen then shouted that they had brought down the parts previously removed from the submarine engines, and that the sub crew could now replace these. The parts were taken out to the sub in the launch. Then the horsemen departed.

Doc Savage said, "That is a break. Give them time to repair the engines."

A small, silent group, they put their faces into the wind and worked along the bay shore. Going was easier close to the water, but spray washed them, and they continually slipped and bruised themselves on wet rocks. The moon had moved over in the sky and its silver eye no longer looked brightly into that part of the pit that was the bay.

There was no watchman at the boat landing. The power launch bobbed madly on the choppy waves of the bay, its nose and stern fast to spring lines, its strake hitting against fenders. Spray traveled over the stone dock in hissing sheets.

Ham said, "If we start the launch motor, they'll hear it."

Doc said, "We'll swim."

"Swim?" Monk gulped. *"Br-r-r!"*

Doc Savage dropped into the water and Monk and Ham followed, sans enthusiasm; the cold water bit them as if it had teeth. The others remained on the dock.

Doc Savage swam out into the bay, trailed by Monk and Ham. It was not easy, but as long as they were careful not to breathe in water, and to dive through the waves, progress was not impossible. The main difficulty was keeping bearings.

Maintaining direction would have been easier if Doc and his aids could have driven directly into the waves, or coasted with them; as it was, they were taking the harder diagonal. Time after time, they had to ride the crests of waves while they relocated their goal.

Climbing on the submarine when they reached it was a problem. For boarding, they selected the bow, because the anchor cable would be making a noise there. Doc Savage made three attempts, got on deck, then hauled Monk and Ham aboard.

Monk and Ham began to shake violently from the cold. When Monk tried to whisper, the best he could manage was something like steam escaping from a small teakettle.

Waves and spray were being carried over the deck by the wind, so deck hatches would be closed. Likely to be open for ventilation was the hatch in the top of the conning tower.

Doc and his aids worked aft, clinging to the rail, and climbed the conning tower ladder, hands so numb from cold that they felt like hooks.

There were half a dozen of the crew aboard the submarine —all having a celebrating drink in a compartment which had a single door. Doc Savage slammed the door shut, got it barred.

DOC SAVAGE then pulled up the motor parts which he and his men had removed on the occasion of their previous escape and hung from an elevator fin by a wire line.

The bronze man seemed in no hurry as he went over the submarine and familiarized himself with its operation, but his appearance of leisure was deception; and it was only a few minutes before he took up a position in the control room. By that time, Monk and Ham had the engines ready.

Doc addressed Monk and Ham, "Both of you get sounding lines," he said, "and take soundings as rapidly as you can while we work in toward the dock."

"Idea is to get the sub as near the dock as we can?" Ham asked.

"Exactly."

Doc Savage turned switches, and the electric motors, ordinarily used for underwater propulsion, began turning over. Closing another switch brought the anchor up quietly enough.

Doc Savage gave the submarine headway enough to make it maneuverable. The wind did not have much effect on the craft, most of its hull being under water.

Monk and Ham took soundings and dashed along the slippery deck in relays to advise him of the water depth. There was good depth almost to the wharf.

Doc put the anchor down, dragged back on it to sink the flukes in the bottom, then used the twin propellers to maneuver the stern around. Finally they were lying close enough to the dock to span the gap with a gangplank. They made fast.

Doc Savage went to Rowe, who had waited on the dock.

"Will men from the village help you?" Doc asked.

"Any guns on that submarine?" Rowe demanded.

"Not only guns, but gas and gas masks."

"Then I won't have any trouble getting help," Rowe said grimly.

Doc Savage gave him the phial containing the liquid that would frighten the dogs. "Have each of your men smear this on himself," Doc instructed. "That will take care of the dogs."

Rowe went away into the windy night.

The rest of Doc's party began getting weapons ready by

unlocking the large rack of automatic rifles. With each rifle was a knapsack of ammunition clips; another rack held grenades as well as gas shells for the submarine's deck guns; and there were different types of gas, each designated by symbols, and also defensive equipment for the gas, consisting of masks and complete rubberized coverall suits.

They did not take any of this stuff ashore, not wanting it where it could be seized in case there was a raid.

"Listen!" Monk exploded suddenly.

Doc Savage had already heard. Men were running. They clattered rocks with their feet, breathed heavily.

"Rowe!" Doc said.

Rowe led a shadowy, panting group of less than a score of men.

"We're blowed up!" Rowe yelled.

Monk growled, "You made enough noise to tip off——"

"They know what we're up to at the castle!" Rowe shouted. "One of the villagers told 'em!"

"What happened?" Doc demanded.

"The three horsemen you overcame regained consciousness!" Rowe snarled. "They offered money, hired one of the villagers to double-cross us. They listened to us telling the village that you were alive and had guns, then they ran to the castle. We tried to head 'em off. We couldn't catch 'em."

Monk called out. The homely chemist had been watching the cliff path that led to the castle, and he had seen lights appear. The lights were blazing torches carried by horsemen who plunged down the path from the castle.

"We're all set for a nice war!" Monk yelled.

They were confronted with a war, rather than set for it. There were over a hundred pirates in the castle, all armed and, with their buccaneering jeopardized, they would be excessively willing to fight. Doc's group did not number a score and a half.

Doc Savage said, "Get aboard the sub!"

THE rush across the gangplank was immediate and enthusiastic. The U-boat symbolized escape from a foe of superior numbers, and in the case of Rowe and his villager allies, of superior willingness to fight.

Not that Rowe and the others did not have their hearts with Doc Savage's plans; it was just that they had been cowed for a long time, and a whipped cur is not immediately turned into a fighting terrier.

Monk and Ham cast off the lines which held the subseas craft to the wharf, and Doc Savage then ran up on the anchor and lifted it. Monk and Ham then stood on deck with automatic rifles, and tried to shoot the launch, forgotten and left tied at the dock, full of holes. They did not, they had to admit, do the launch much damage.

Dashing forward, they got the cover off the handiest dock gun. When they examined the gun, their hearts fell. They uncovered all the big deck rifles. Essential parts of the breech mechanism had been removed from each.

Monk reported this to Doc Savage and added, "That's bad!"

It was bad. The launch was big, more of a motor yacht than a launch, and faster than the submarine. It could easily overtake them.

Doc Savage said, "We had better go back and smash the launch."

They went back, but they did not smash the launch, because the riders from the castle got to the wharf first. Some of them sprang into the launch and got it in the clear. Those left on shore peppered the sub with rifle bullets. The slugs could not puncture the submarine hull, but they made a disturbing racket.

Doc Savage backed the submarine out into the little bay again. They could not stay on deck because of the rifle bullets. Through the periscope, they saw the launch swerve back to the wharf, and hang there while objects the size of kegs were loaded aboard.

Monk aimed the searchlight at the wharf, then got under cover, and Doc switched the light on. He pointed it by steering the sub, and the light brightened the wharf enough that they could see what was going on.

"That's bad!" Ham gasped.

"Depth bombs!" Monk croaked. "They're loadin' depth bombs on that launch!"

Just then, a stream of bullets from a machine gun on shore hit the searchlight, smashing it.

There was a thump. A fountain of water jumped up fifty feet high to the left of the sub.

"Rowe!" Doc called.

Rowe came running, just as another fountain of water jumped up, closer this time.

"Field gun," Doc said.

"Yes, a field gun!" Rowe admitted. "They must have brought one down from the castle!"

Doc Savage aimed the submarine for the mouth of the harbor.

"Give the diesels full speed ahead," he directed.

THE submarine plowed toward the sea. The launch fell in behind. Two machine guns on the launch licked their noses with red, and tracer bullets waved around like strange sparkling strings. Monk and Ham began sharpshooting with rifles, and the launch dropped back.

The field gun coughed a blast that reddened the cliffs, and the shell dug up water. The submarine could escape its menace bu submerging; but if they submerged, there was the launch and its depth bombs.

Doc Savage called Rowe and asked him about the harbor mouth channel.

"It's pretty bad," Rowe said. "How much water does this thing draw?"

"About twenty-five feet," Doc told him. "We're running with the decks submerged to make a small target for that field gun."

"Get in close to the west cliff," Rowe said. "Get so close to the cliff that you think you'll hit it. The deep water is there."

They ran in so close to the cliff that it seemed to lean out over the submarine.

It was then that the field gun hit them. It was a lucky strike, because the sub conning tower was a small target, and the shell opened the after portion like a tin can. There was a blinding flash, and the effect of a hammer striking their heads.

Incoming water rushed against the bronze man and carried him down into the lower control room. He fell all of a dozen feet and struck hard steel; but that shock, after the shock of the shell bursting, seemed something of no importance.

Chapter XIX

PIRATE'S PATH

THERE was, except for the rush of incoming water, a moment of silence in the submarine. Then Portia screamed, and that cry was like a baton wave that set off a hideous orchestration of frightened howling.

More as a sleepwalker than a coordinating human being, Doc Savage dragged himself to the panel and set the controls to blow the buoyancy tanks. Watching the instrument dials show that compressed air was going into the tanks was like taking a breath after being trapped under water.

Doc Savage got to the emergency controls. The submarine had two sets of controls, those outside on the sheltered conning tower for surface travel, and those below for underwater navigation. The compasses and everything else were intact, although there was water a yard deep on the floor, and more coming in.

But less water was coming, and finally it stopped, the submarine having risen enough.

Monk and Ham were giving the fear-stricken islanders pieces of their minds in loud, but calm voices. They got them quieted down. Then they came into the control room, just as there was another grating crash, and a jar, and Doc Savage knew the submarine had drifted against the cliff.

"Monk, take the wheel!" Doc ordered.

The bronze man then climbed up into the wrecked conning tower to see what chance they had. The sub bow was against the cliff. It struck again.

"Reverse engines!" Doc said.

The submarine backed away, then got headway again, and pushed out of the mouth of the bay. Rifle bullets kept hitting the craft. The submarine lifted, sank, rolled and plunged in the huge seas. Doc Savage held to a twisted pipe. Salt water doused him by barrelfuls.

The U-boat was clear of the harbor mouth.

"Port helm!" the bronze man directed.

It was a necessity to get the cliff between themselves and the field gun. The submarine angled over, lurching.

"That's far enough," Doc said. "Pass up tear gas."

THE men began passing up the gas. The stuff was in grenades.

"Only tear gas!" Doc warned.

He set the bombs to explode, then tossed them out on the submarine deck where the gale would catch the vapor and carry it back to those on the launch.

It was unlikely those on the launch had gas masks. They would be blinded. They would have to turn back, and turn back before they were totally unable to see. This was no kind of sea in which to be sightless in such a small craft.

Then Rowe came scrambling up out of the innards of the sub. He was nursing two grenades in his arms, having trouble climbing.

"Last of the tear gas!" he screamed.

Then he jerked the firing pins and heaved the grenades out on deck.

Not until Doc Savage saw one of Rowe's grenades, lying spewing in the steaming water on the moonlit deck, did he realize what Rowe was doing. He jumped for the man, but Rowe got rid of the other grenade.

Doc Savage made a move to go out on deck. But he could accomplish nothing, and he might kill himself. For it was poison gas that Rowe had thrown out there.

Doc seized Rowe.

"I told you *tear gas!*" he shouted.

Water sheeted over them as a wave broke on the submarine. Rowe's voice was hard to understand, but it was triumphant.

"You could say tear gas!" he grated. "You haven't been tortured by them for two years!"

Fortunately, there was enough wind to carry Rowe's poison gas away from the submarine.

Doc Savage was troubled. He had never taken human lives directly; always he had done all he could to prevent any one dying in connection with anything that he was doing. He had made that his unalterable policy from the first. He would adhere to it.

He got a flashlight and tried to signal a warning, by blinking to the launch. The men on the craft fired with a machine gun, and he had to get down.

A few moments later, bullets stopped coming from the launch. Doc Savage exposed himself to look.

The launch had turned half around, and was running off at a tangent, although it still held speed. It rolled amazingly. Waves broke over it.

From the erratic way it acted, Doc knew the steersman had gone down from Rowe's poison gas. The huge waves and terrific wind carried the launch back against the rocky cliffs of the island.

Doc and his aids never did know whether the men on the launch died from Rowe's gas, or were drowned, or were blown to pieces when the depth bombs let loose. They found some parts of the launch floating, and two bodies; but that was four days later. Rocks and sharks had done too much damage to the bodies to make an autopsy feasible.

An autopsy would have been rather foolish, anyway. As Monk said, a jury wouldn't be likely to do much to Rowe.

ALL knew, before the four days elapsed and they found the bodies, that both Prince Albert and Henry had been aboard the launch.

Before they found that out, though, they removed prisoners from the submarine compartment, threw the fear of things hereafter into them, and persuaded the captives to tell that the breech parts from the deck guns were hidden between the storage batteries in the bilge.

Having made the deck rifles usable, and waited for dawn, when the gale subsided, Doc's party pegged a few explosive shells at the castle, and blew away one corner. Later, they landed Rowe and his islanders, armed with rifles, tear gas and gas masks, and covered their bushwhacking form of attack.

It was about two o'clock in the afternoon when some one waved a sheet from a rifle barrel on the castle walls.

On the theory that the island was a possession of England as much as anybody, Doc Savage summoned a British warship, after they got the submarine radio working.

Treasure taken by piracy was stored in subterranean rooms below the castle. They would have been surprised to find it anywhere else.

The lack of a great store of loot was a surprise and a puzzle until they had questioned their prisoners, who were willing to admit that most of the cash taken off ships lay in banks in Europe and America. Among Prince Albert's effects, Doc found a list of the deposits.

Monk and Ham, for once, got along rather well. They had located their two pets, the pig and the dwarf ape, in the castle, so they were happy enough on that score.

The frosting on Monk and Ham's cake, however, was that each had a very attractive young woman to pursue. Each one considered himself rather a hand at that sort of thing.

Usually, they laid suit to the same young lady, and fought like cats and dogs over the affair. This time, there was enough feminine pulchritude to go around.

Ham campaigned intensively for the Duchess Portia, who seemed to have been cured of thrill-seeking, and in a mood for another whirl at domestic bliss.

Monk devoted his attentions to China, and the tall, attractive showgirl was not unresponsive.

A WEEK later, when the British warship had taken the pirates and their loot aboard, and was waiting for Doc Savage and the others, Doc had a visit from Monk and Ham.

Monk and Ham seemed unexpectedly friendly with each other. They looked, in fact, as if they had been mutually sympathizing. They also appeared apprehensive.

"Doc," Monk said earnestly, "both Portia and China admire you."

"Exactly," Ham agreed. "Both young women regard you very highly."

Doc Savage was puzzled. "What is this leading up to?" he asked.

"With encouragement," Monk muttered, "the young women might fall for you."

"In fact," Ham groaned, "they've got to!"

Doc said, "I do not get this."

"Look at us!" Monk commanded.

Doc looked at them. Except for a large case of jitters, there seemed to be nothing wrong.

"You're looking," Monk explained, "at two prospective bridegrooms."

"Congratulations," Doc said.

"Congratulations, nothing!" Ham wailed. "We don't want to get married! Doc, you've got to steal our girls away from us! Make love to 'em! Make 'em forget us!"

Doc Savage pondered this dubiously. "You'd better find another thief," he said at last.

Monk and Ham groaned.

"Come on, Ham," Monk muttered, "let's proposition some of them snappy-lookin' officers on that battleship."

To the world at large, Doc Savage is a strange, mysterious figure of glistening bronze skin and golden eyes. To his fans he is the greatest adventure hero of all time, whose fantastic exploits are unequaled for hair-raising thrills, breathtaking escapes, blood-curdling excitement!

- ☐ H5729 THE TERROR IN THE NAVY (60¢)
- ☐ S7102 HAUNTED OCEAN (75¢)
- ☐ H4879 FANTASTIC ISLAND (60¢)
- ☐ H5326 QUEST OF QUI (60¢)
- ☐ H5298 THE SECRET IN THE SKY (60¢)
- ☐ H5285 DEATH IN SILVER (60¢)
- ☐ H5422 THE SQUEAKING GOBBLINS (60¢)
- ☐ H4707 HEX (60¢)
- ☐ H4065 RED SNOW (60¢)
- ☐ H4721 WORLD'S FAIR GOBLIN (60¢)
- ☐ H4624 THE DAGGER IN THE SKY (60¢)
- ☐ H4689 MERCHANTS OF DISASTER (60¢)
- ☐ H4730 THE GOLD OGRE (60¢)
- ☐ H4761 THE MAN WHO SHOOK THE EARTH (60¢)
- ☐ H4810 THE SEA MAGICIAN (60¢)
- ☐ S5991 THE PIRATE'S GHOST (75¢)
- ☐ S5947 THE LIVING FIRE MENACE (75¢)
- ☐ S5909 THE MAJII (75¢)
- ☐ S6542 THE SUBMARINE MYSTERY (75¢)

8 amazing Doc Savage escapades in a boxed set!

- ☐ K5136 The Fantastic Adventures of Doc Savage ($6.00)

Bantam Books, Inc., Dept. DS, Room 2450, 666 Fifth Ave., New York, N. Y. 10019

Please send me the merchandise I have indicated.

Name_____

Address_____

City_____State_____Zip Code_____

(Please send check or money order. No currency or C.O.D.'s. Add 10¢ per book on orders of less than 5 books to cover the cost of postage and handling.)

Please allow about four weeks for delivery.   DS—8/71